Frederick Saunders

The Story of Some Famous Books

Frederick Saunders

The Story of Some Famous Books

ISBN/EAN: 9783744748285

Printed in Europe, USA, Canada, Australia, Japan

Cover: Foto ©Andreas Hilbeck / pixelio.de

More available books at **www.hansebooks.com**

THE STORY

OF

SOME FAMOUS BOOKS

BY

FREDERICK SAUNDERS

Author of "Salad for the Solitary and the Social,"
"Evenings with the Sacred Poets," "Pastime
Papers," etc.

LONDON
ELLIOT STOCK, 62 PATERNOSTER ROW
1887

PREFACE.

"IF a secret history of books could be written," said Thackeray, "and the author's private thoughts and meanings noted down alongside of his story, how many insipid volumes would become interesting, and dull tales excite the reader!" It was this suggestive remark of the great novelist that prompted the present attempt to group together the following notes and incidents illustrative of this subject. These notes have been garnered from a somewhat desultory though extended course of reading and research; yet they are far from being exhaustive of the subject. They are necessarily brief, but should *they, in any instance, be regarded as insufficient, the remark attributed to an eminent French writer may possibly be urged as apologetic : he said, " The multiplicity of facts and writings has become so great, that everything soon will have to be reduced to extracts." It has been also urged that "so great is the mass of our book-heritage, that it is absolutely impossible for anyone to make himself acquainted with even the hundredth part of it : so that our choice lies for the most part between ignorance of much that we would like to know, and that kind of acquaintance which is to be acquired only by desultory reading." And since it has been affirmed that " he is the best author who gives the reader the most knowledge and takes from him the least time," these claims have not been ignored, it is believed, in the preparation of the following pages. Everett has remarked that "many of the best books have been written by persons who at the time of writing them had no intention of becoming authors,"—as in the instance of Pope's "Rape of the Lock" and Rogers's "Pleasures of Memory." Locke, when he began his work on the "Human Understanding," thought it would not exceed a few sheets. Often the consciousness of talents and abilities for such work seems to have been concealed from their possessors until some incident has proved the occasion of their development. Besides this, there is a joy in writing which none but writers know—" a pleasure in poetic pains;" and in this consists their genius. Montaigne evidently wrote from such an impulse, since his writings are not only in the manner but in the spirit of a monologue. Many other writers might be added to the category,—Lamb, Hazlitt, Leigh Hunt, De Quincey, and others. In many instances the birth of a book may be traceable to some exciting incident, like many of our discoveries in art and science. Again, it seems as if an inspiration came to the mind,—*

> *" Great thoughts, great feelings came to them,*
> *Like instincts, unawares !"*

Carlyle pays a generous but just tribute to literary toilers—himself foremost of the noble order—in the following energetic sentences :—" Among these men are to be found the brightest specimens and the chief benefactors of mankind. It is they who keep awake the finer parts of our souls, that give better aims than power or pleasure, and withstand the total sovereignty of mammon on this earth. They are the vanguard in the march of mind, the intellectual backwoodsmen, re-claiming from the idle wilderness new territories for thought and activity. Pity, that from all their conquests, so rich in benefit to others, themselves should reap so little. Of all the things which man can do or make here below, by far the most momentous, wonderful, and worthy, are the things we call books." Emerson has justly remarked that "they prize books most who are themselves wise,"—since they know by experience, that books not only minister to our purest intellectual enjoyment, but they also invigorate, ennoble, and enrich the mind, as well as beguile us of the rough and rugged paths of life. Theirs is the talismanic spell to

> " Lift us unawares
> Out of our meaner cares."

                       F. S.

CONCERNING THE HONOUR OF BOOKS.

SINCE honour from the honourer proceeds,
How well do they deserve, that memorize
And leave in books for all posterities
The names of worthies and their virtuous deeds;
When all their glory else, like water-weeds
Without their element, presently dies,
And all their greatness quite forgotten lies,
And when and how they flourished no man heeds.
How poor remembrances are statues, tombs,
And other monuments that men erect
To princes, which remain in closèd rooms
Where but a few behold them, in respect
Of Books, that to the universal eye
Show how they lived, the other where they lie.

JOHN FLORIO (1545—1625).

CONTENTS.

THE STORY

OF

SOME FAMOUS BOOKS.

I.

INTRODUCTORY. — CHAUCER. — SPENSER. —SIDNEY'S "ARCADIA."

A S introductory to an essay on the origin of books, it may not be deemed irrelevant to allude for a moment to the origin of authors. Horace Smith insists that

" Were there no readers there certainly would be no writers; clearly, therefore, the existence of writers depends upon the existence of readers; and, of course, since the cause must be antecedent to the effect, readers existed before writers. Yet, on the other hand, if there were no writers there could be no readers; so it would appear that writers must be antecedent to readers."

Here there seems to be no sophistry, but a clear logical sequence ; and yet one is hardly ready to accept the conclusion of the argument. I think, indeed, there certainly would be writers even if there were no readers. Before leaving authors for books, something should be said about that strange class of writers who have for ages been accustomed to send adrift over the world their literary offspring, and leave them in a condition of orphanage, unprotected, and exposed to all the casualties and contingencies of time. What a concourse of literary fugitives are ever hovering about, or seen nestled in some "poet's corner" of a periodical, or found fluttering out their brief butterfly existence in the columns of some newspaper. Some of these waifs are of strange and surprising beauty, and merit better treatment and conservation. These fugitives and strays of the pen have been classed under a generic name or patronymic, and as Douglas Jerrold has admirably written all that need be said about their mysterious cognomen, herewith I present his words on the subject :—

"Of *Anon.* but little is known, although his works are excessively numerous; for this mysterious writer seems to have dabbled in almost every variety of topic, both in prose and verse; from the cloudy heights of philosophy down to the commonplace things of everyday life. Not confined to any country or creed, his name confronts us in books and periodicals, English, American, French, and German. If all the productions of this prolific scribe were collected together, they would, doubtless, require for their reception something like the capacity of a British Museum. He must, also, be the most modest of authors, to have done so much for literature and the world, and yet so persistently to have preserved his incognito. The only writer who may in the least compete with him in fecundity and personal mystery is his contemporary, *Ibid.*"

It may seem trite at the present day to apostrophise books when they are in almost every person's hands; but all books are not true and good books, or such as win the scholar's choice.

Books are no longer inscribed on illuminated parchments, and kept secluded in the cloistered cell of monasteries, as in times of yore; but we live in a day when, instead of having laboriously to pore over the verbose manuscripts of antique lore, we have presented to us the golden grain of knowledge winnowed from the chaff; and this immunity is offered to all. Not only in the chamber of the scholar, therefore, should we seek for the fruits of study and reading, but the cottage of the farmer and artisan should also bear evidence of the beneficial results of the study of good books. The truest blessing of literature is found in the inward light and peace which it bestows. It has been justly remarked that

"Genius has its nectaries and its delicate glands, and secretions of sweetness, and upon these the thoughtful reader dilates. A good book resembles a fruitful orchard-tree, carefully tended; its fruits are perennial, and the better with age."

Said Blanco White, the author of one of the finest sonnets we have :—

"If I open the treasures of literature, which nourished my mind in youth, I feel young again, and my mind seems to be transported into the regions of love and beauty, which I can now better enjoy than during the fever of the passions."

The books we love, like our personal friends, exert an influence over our minds, and we cherish the memory of our intercourse with them both, with pleasure ever afterwards. To many a student, who prefers quiet retirement to the noisy excitement of the crowded resorts of fashionable life, his favourite books will have thus acquired for him a personality. He may not be without his personal friendships, yet he will doubtless repeat the experience of Bonnivard, without his enforced seclusion :—

> " My books and I grew friends,
> So much a long communion tends
> To make us what we are ; even I
> Regained my freedom with a sigh."

Mr. Lowell wisely urges concentration and definiteness of purpose,—the choice not merely of the best, but of some one great author, the reading and study of whose writings will quicken attention, force upon us the necessity of thinking, and open up many suggestions of other reading, associated with and centring in the author or the subject of investigation first chosen.

Books are often spoken of as companions. But they may be good or bad companions. Mr. Lowell extends the old adage that a man is known by the company he keeps, and affirms that he is also made by it. Readers, young or old, may profitably heed what he says in this connection :—

"There is a choice in books as in friends, and the mind sinks or rises to the level of its habitual society, is subdued, as Shakespeare says of the dyer's hand, to what it works in. Cato's advice, 'Cum bonis ambula' (Consort with the good), is quite as true if we extend it to books, for they, too, insensibly give away their own nature to the mind that converses with them. They either beckon upward or drag down."

Tuckerman has well said :—

"It is remarkable that the men whose relish for books is the most keen, who read sympathetically, not merely to store the memory and weave the ties of familiar and endearing association with beloved authors, should invariably repudiate the idea of an extensive library. Thinkers do not require books for the information they convey so much as stimulants and faithful companions. They can generate ideas for themselves, and take up a volume, as they turn to a friend, for the refreshment of sympathy or attrition of mind."

Let us imagine a student anxious to be instructed in all that has been done and thought in preceding times. Whither shall he go? If he betake himself to nature, he finds that all impress written thereon by man has been eaten out by the corroding tooth of time. He gropes laboriously amid physical relics, but a vague and partial glimpse is his only reward. He visits his library, however, and presents the talisman of a book, and the heralds of discovery come forth to greet him. Galileo holds to his eye the magical mechanism that draws within its range the rings of Saturn and the satellites of Jupiter. He looks again, and Torricelli makes the heavy mercury the prophet of the storm. Again, and the needle, quivering to an influence too subtle to be traced, points unerringly amidst the solitudes of the sea. Harvey tells him why the crimson mounts into the cheek; Jenner panoplies him against his most direful foe, and Daguerre commands the pencil of the sun. He turns again, and Locke teaches him the secrets of his own mind; Bacon instructs him in the true mode of study; Linnæus spreads before him the beauties of leaf and flower; Lyell clips off some crust from the ancient rock, and reads the earth's autobiography; while Newton and La Place bear him safely along the starry pavement of the Milky Way. Deny these treasured resources to the poet, the historian, and the student, and the long-buried ages are voiceless and un-instructive. But by the magic of books, the son of science is rapt by a problem, the philosopher by an abstruse speculation, the antiquary is carried centuries back into the chivalric past, and the lover of poesy is borne upon glittering wings into the regions of imagination and fancy.

"Why should it not be a worthy end, as old Sir John saith, to read simply for delight?" it has been asked.

"God dangles peaches before our eyes, and spreads flowers beneath our feet, and fills the earth with colours and forms of beauty as well as the air with sounds of sweetest melody; and He no more means us to discard the delightsome from our course of reading, than banish strawberries from our tables, or flowers from our writing-tables."

How wonderful is the embalmed essence of volatile thought in a book! Think of the Homeric ballads. Their author's earthly existence ceased three thousand years since; his body reverted to dust; but his immortal work outlives all the mutations of Time.

Said Thomas Hood :—

" Experience enables me to depose to the comfort and blessing that literature can prove in seasons of sickness and sorrow ;—how powerfully intellectual pursuits can help in keeping the head from crazing and the heart from breaking."

And Madame de Genlis tells us that she had never tasted pleasures so true as those she found " in the study of books, in writing or in music." What can supply their place ?

" The vision and the faculty Divine " is the endowment of a fickle and capricious goddess, for she comes not responsively alike to all her devotees. To some, the inspiration, or Divine afflatus, lights up the chambers of the mind, and, like the electric current, not only illumines but energises its powers. To others, the gift has to be sought by ingenious and persevering effort, by earnest study, and sudorous brain-toil. Some win the rewards of fame for their toil, but others, again, fail to secure the applause of the world, and for the pleasure they have

given, have, but too often in return, been
denied the necessities of life. Homer,
for instance, was the first poet and beggar
of note among the ancients ; and in later
times, Cervantes died of hunger, like
Otway, and some others.

Southey was not endowed with too
much money, but he worked on nobly
and unselfishly to the last,—until his
mind gave way; finding happiness and
joy in the pursuit of letters; "not so
learned as poor, not so poor as proud,
and not so proud as happy!" These
were his own fine words.

Sir Walter Scott was another, and even
more illustrious, instance of the love
of letters under the most formidable
of difficulties. The sacrifices and efforts
which he made during the last few years
of his eventful life, even while paralysed,
and scarcely able to hold his pen, exhibit
him in a truly heroic light. When his
physician remonstrated with him against
his excessive brain-work, he replied, "If I
were to be idle, I should go mad!"

Johnson was a poor man, but a very
brave one : his head was full of learning,

but his pockets were often empty. His bluff and gruff exterior covered a kindly and noble nature. How many more such examples exist on the scroll of literary fame ?

" Authors are beings only half of earth,—
    They own a world apart from other men :
A glorious realm, given by their fancy birth,
    Subjects, a sceptre, and a diadem :
A fairy land of thought in which sweet bliss
    Would run to ecstasy in wild delight—
But that stern Nature drags them back to this
    With call imperious, which they may not
      slight :
And then they traffic with their thoughts, to live,
    And coin their labouring brains for daily bread :
Getting scant dross, for the rich ore they give,—
    While often with the gift their life is shed !
And thus they die, leaving behind a name
    At once their country's glory and her shame ! " [1]

" The mental powers acquire their full robust-ness when the cheek loses its ruddy hue, and the limbs their elastic step," wrote Dr. Guthrie, " and pale thought sits on mánly brows, and the student's lamp burns far into the silent night. The finest flowers of genius have grown in an atmosphere where those of nature are prone to droop, and difficult to bring to maturity."

[1] Fred. West.

Prince, a self-taught poet of England, thus portrays a literary laboratory :—

"Lo ! in that quiet and contracted room,
Where the lone lamp just mitigates the gloom,
Sits a pale student—stirred with high desires,
With lofty principles and gifted fires ;—
From time to time, with calm, enquiring looks,
He culls the ore of wisdom from his books ;—
Clears it, sublimes it, till it flows refined
From his alembic crucible of mind."

Mind lives by mind ; thoughts germinate their kind. We see this alike in the reproductions of nature and in the inexorable demands of the physical system for its appropriate food.

"Every one of my writings," Goethe says, "has been furnished to me by a thousand different persons, a thousand different things ; the learned and the ignorant, the wise and the foolish,—without having the least suspicion of it,—to bring me the offering of their thoughts, their faculties, their experience. Often others have sowed the harvest I have reaped."

Great results are the sure rewards of the toil of study and persevering mental industry. Talents, however brilliant, cannot supersede reading and thinking ; and thinking assimilates what we read, so that it becomes our own. Aristotle distinguished the learned and the unlearned as the living and the dead.

" The authors truly remembered and loved are men in the best sense of the term ;—the human, the individual informs and stamps their books with an image, or an affluence not born of will, or mere ingenuity, but emanating from the soul ;—and this is the quality that endears and perpetuates their fame. Hence Goldsmith is beloved, Milton reverenced, and the grave of Burns a ' Mecca of the mind.' There are books, as there are pictures, which do not catch the thoughtless eye, and yet are the gems of the virtuoso, the oracles of the philosopher, and the consolations of the poet. We love authors, as we love individuals, according to our affinities ; and the extent of the popular appreciation is no more a standard to us, than the world's estimate of our friend, whose nature we have tested by faithful companionship and sympathetic intercourse. He who has not the mental independence to be loyal to his own intellectual benefactors, is as much a heathen as one who repudiates his natural kin ; indeed, an honest soul clings more tenaciously to neglected merit in authors, as in men ; there is a chivalry of taste as of manners. Doubtless Lamb's test for the old English dramatists, Addison's admiration of Milton's poetry, and Carlyle's devotion to Goethe, were all the more earnest and keen because they were ignored by their neighbours. It is well to obey these decided idiosyncrasies." [1]

[1] Tuckerman.

Among the numerous instances in which the world is indebted to seeming accident for the development of latent genius, the following might be cited, as illustrative. Malebranche, once loitering in a bookstore in Paris, happened to see a volume entitled *L'Homme*, by Descartes, which work he took home and read. It is to this incident that we are to ascribe those compositions in metaphysics and morals that have placed him in the front rank of the writers of his age. For another illustration in point we might refer to Cowley, who in his early days chanced to meet with a copy of Spenser's *Faerie Queen*, with the beauties of which he became so enchanted that forthwith he became himself a poet. Who will venture to affirm that we are not indebted to Shakespeare's leaving his native town for London, and engaging with a company of actors for the purpose of aiding his father's resources, that our literature has been so enriched and glorified with his matchless creations?

It was remarked by D'Israeli that "had several of our first writers set their fortunes on the cast of their friends' opinions, we might have lost some precious compositions."

The friends of Thomson discovered nothing but faults in his early productions, one of which happened to be his noblest, the *Winter.* He had created a new school of art, and appealed from his circle to the public. It was Gibbon who wrote :—

" I was disgusted with the modest practice of reading the manuscript to my friends. Of such friends some will praise for politeness and some will criticise for vanity."

And Montaigne has honestly told us that in his own province they considered that for him to attempt to become an author was perfectly ludicrous. "While at a distance," he says, " printers purchase me, at home I am compelled to purchase printers." Much more might be cited of a similar character, to show the discouraging influence of prejudice and hypercriticism at the commencement of a literary career; but in spite of all, genius will triumph over adverse conditions, notwithstanding all the depressing moods and tenses which accompany literary composition.

"Poetry is its own exceeding great reward," said Coleridge. "It soothes afflictions, crowns poverty, rocks asleep cares and sickness, multiplies and refines pleasures, and endears solitude. We think of Milton, after the sight of his eyes had gone from him, when the rays of early studies shone across his path ; when the voices he loved in youth—solemn notes of tragic, or livelier numbers of lyric verse—stole into his ear out of the gloom; and nightingales sang as sweetly in Cripplegate, as when the April leaf trembled in his father's garden."

We remember Camoens in all his trials, —whether gazing on land and water from that rocky chair built by nature for him, and still called by his name, upon an isthmus of the China seas; shipwrecked, with his *Lusiad* held above the waves, and drifting upon a plank to shore ; in Lisbon, waiting in solitude and darkness the return of a black servant, who helped to feed his hunger with the alms he begged ; or closing his eyes, a sick mendicant and outcast, in a public hospital. We weep with Tasso, in the hospital of St. Anna, scared by the screams of maniacs in the neighbouring cells, yet sometimes turning his thoughts to the correction of the Eastern Story, and peopling the loneliness

with the magnificent tumult of a crusade.
What upheld the buffeted pilgrims of
Fame in their struggle and poverty? An
animating mastering sense of music lived
in their hearts, finding utterance in tones
more lulling than the south-west wind of
the " Arcadia," which in the ear of Sidney
crept "over flowery fields and shadowed
waters in the heat of summer." Happy
eyes that make pictures when they are
shut ! We are told by naturalists that
birds of Paradise fly best against the wind ;
and so the many of the votaries of the
muse " learn in suffering what they teach
in song."[1]

Who, looking back upon their glorious
age, does not respond to Whittier's poetic
words ?—

> "I love the old melodious lays
>   Which softly melt the ages through,
>   The songs of Spenser's golden days,
>   Arcadian Sidney's silver phrase
> Sprinkling our noon of time with freshest morn-
>   ing dew."

The Elizabethan age boasted a wealth
of learning unequalled by any preced-

[1] Willmott.

ing and subsequent epoch in the history of letters. Shakespeare, surrounded as he was by heroes and mighty men of intellect, formed the great central sun around which the lesser orbs revolved. It was one of their number that justly remarked, referring to the magnates in theology, as well as the great poets of that time, that "good men were the stars of the world, and that our poets were also the priesthood interpreting the great problem of human life, with its mysteries, passions, and destiny."

The great era of the discovery of America, and the important events which synchronized with it,—the invention of the printing-press and the revival of learning,—present the natural starting-point in the history of our literature, and consequently the production of books. Till then, scholarship was, for the most part, restricted to the cloister, and even the great writers of classic times were well-nigh forgotten amid the polemical discussions of the monastic schools. Without were barbarism, storm and darkness, and the tumult of war ; within were yet a few devoted ones to tend the lamp of learning, and " amid light, fragrance, and music, the ritual of genius continued to be solemnized." Thus the sacred fire of learning burst forth from its scattered shrines, until torch after torch illumined the civilised world. It was most fitting that the " art preservative of arts " should be inaugurated with the printing of the " Book of books," since no other book—apart from its Divine authority— has furnished such innumerable themes for historians, poets, philosophers, moral. ists, and teachers of its doctrines, as the Bible.

Of the *Mazarin Bible* it is well to note that its discovery was almost accidental. Debure, the celebrated bibliographer, states that mere chance led him to discover this literary treasure,—the firstfruits of the printing art, and the most precious of books. He says :—

" When making some explorations in the library of the Cardinal, we were not a little surprised to find this first and most celebrated work of the press, which a simple impulse of curiosity caused us to open."

The existence of such a work was, however, suspected, from the allusion to it in the *Chronicle of Cologne*, which speaks of the jubilee year 1450, when the first book, a Bible, "of the larger type," was discovered.

In these rambling researches over the wide and varied domain of our vernacular literature, in quest of some brief notices of famous books, I solicit the reader's indulgence, at the outset, on account of the desultory and fragmentary character of my notes and details.

By common consent, the critics assign the post of honour to Geoffrey Chaucer, as father of the English muse; it is fitting, therefore, that he should claim our first attention, especially as he is also the pioneer of an illustrious succession of British bards; or as Campbell, in his poetic phrase, apostrophises him :—

" Our Helicon's first fountain stream !
　　Our morning-star of song,—that led the
　　　way
　　To welcome the long-after coming beam
　　　Of Spenser's light, and Shakespeare's
　　　　perfect day ! "

Chaucer in his early days devoted himself to French and Italian models; but he subsequently fell back upon his own instincts, and produced works which gave him a claim to be called the first English poet. He did, indeed,

> " Prelude those melodious bursts which fill
> The spacious times of great Elizabeth
> With sounds that echo still."

Chaucer is said so far to have resembled Petrarch that, like him, he was at once poet, scholar, courtier, statesman, and man of the world; but considered merely as poets, the two were the very antipodes of each other. Chaucer might be styled, although living in a rude age, the poet of the affections,—few writers having ever excelled him for his animated portraits, as well as for beautiful passages relating to or inspired by woman. To this proclivity of the tender passion we may ascribe much of his poetry. After a protracted courtship he espoused the lady of his love,— Philippa Picard. It seems to be the concurrent opinion of scholars that little is hazarded in assuming that his *Canterbury Tales* was, as to plan and method, suggested by the *Decameron* of Boccacio. This work of Chaucer was the product of his genius in its full maturity; and although over five centuries have elapsed since the noble work was written, and notwithstanding its obsoleteness of style, it has never been more popular with scholars than it is at the present day. There is, indeed, " an added charm in its antiquity, —something picturesque in it." Chaucer seems to have surrendered himself to the inspiring influences of nature, and revelled, as at a festival, amid birds and flowers; hence the rich arabesque character of his poetry, and the marvellous freshness and bloom of his pastoral pictures. The minstrel may also have derived material for his work from Dante's *Divina Commedia*, as his quotations from it seem to show. The Prologue to the *Canterbury Tales* introduces us to a company of pilgrims, twenty-nine in number, who have met at the *Tabard*, an inn at Southwark (but now no longer standing). There they are entertained by the host on the evening prior to their commencing pilgrimage to the shrine of Thomas à Becket, in

Canterbury Cathedral; and these "sondry folke," by way of beguiling time, agree among themselves to contribute each a tale. These "tales" are such masterly pictures of life in Chaucer's days, that they have justly elicited the following beautiful tribute :—

" Old England's fathers live in Chaucer's lay,
As if they ne'er had died : he grouped and drew
    Their likeness with a spirit of life so gay,
That still they live and breathe, in fancy's view,
Fresh beings fraught with truth's imperishable
        hue ! "

Another instance of the inspiration of the muse by the witching power of beauty was that of Edmund Spenser, since it is known that the first development of his genius was owing to such influence. To the memory of his Rosalind's rare beauty, to the long-felt influence of this first passion, and to the melancholy shade which his early disappointment cast over a mind naturally cheerful, we owe some of the most tender and beautiful passages scattered through his later poems. In like manner, Sir Philip Sidney had caught his poetic fire from the glowing eyes of his

"Stella," and that hapless gallant, the Earl of Surrey, from the fascinations of his fair "Geraldine." Referring to the master-passion, Emerson said :—

"No man ever forgot the visitation of that power to his heart and brain which created all things new—which was the dawn in him of music, poetry, and art—which made the face of Nature radiant with purple light—the morning and the night varied enchantments."

The plan of Spenser's *Faerie Queen* is described in his prefatory letter to Sir Walter Raleigh. The twelve books were to tell the warfare of twelve knights, in whom the twelve virtues of Aristotle were represented. Only six of these books have descended to us ; the rest, if ever written, were supposed to have been destroyed in the fire which occurred at Spenser's castle in Ireland. It was here, in 1589, that he composed the first three books, and then read them to Raleigh, who was so delighted with the poem that he brought Spenser to England, and the Queen, the Court, and the literary world were equally pleased—it being the first great ideal poem yet produced. Raleigh introduced Spenser to Queen Elizabeth, and Campbell thus alludes to this meeting :—

"The fancy might even be pardoned for a momentary superstition, that the genius of their country hovered unseen over their meeting, casting her first look of regard on the poet that was destined to inspire her future Milton, and the other on the maritime hero who paved the way for colonizing distant regions of the earth, where the language of England was to be spoken, and the poetry of Spenser to be admired."

The gallant but unfortunate Sir Walter Raleigh's history is replete with touching interest. The following lines, supposed to be the last he ever wrote, possess all the more interest for the fact of their being found written in his Bible, on the evening preceding his execution :—

"Even such is Time, that takes on trust
Our youth, our joys, our all we have,
And pays us but with age and dust ;
Who in the dark and silent grave,
When we have wandered all our ways,
Shuts up the story of our days :
But from this earth, this grave, this dust,
My God shall raise me up, I trust !"

Spenser, who has been justly styled the "Poet's poet," has been the inspiration of many poets of succeeding ages—of Milton among others. Cowley, when a boy, read the *Faerie Queen*, and became "irrevocably a poet." He was Dryden's master in English. Pope was enthusiastic over it, so were Collins, Gray, Thomson, Wordsworth, Byron, Shelley, and Keats.

The following anecdote by Pope respecting his work is related by Spence:—

"After reading a canto of Spenser two or three days ago to an old lady, she said that I had been showing her a gallery of pictures. I don't know how it is, but she said right, there is something in Spenser that pleases one as strongly in one's old age as it did in one's youth. I read the *Faerie Queen* when I was about twelve, with infinite delight; and I think it gave me as much when I read it over a year or two ago."

This great work on which Spenser's fame rests had been begun at an early stage of his career, and was, it seems, slighted on account of its ethics. Subsequently, in a conversation with some friends, one of them complained that no English poet had given the teachings and precepts of Aristotle and Plato in English verse, and turning to Spenser, said:—

" It is you, sir, to whom it pertaineth to show yourself courteous now unto us all, and to make us beholding unto you for the pleasure and profit which we shall gather from your speeches, if you shall vouchsafe to open unto us the goodly cabinet in which this excellent treasure of virtues lieth locked up from the vulgar sort. . . .' 'I doubt not,' answered Spenser, 'but with the consent of most part of you, I shall be excused at this time of this task which would be laid upon me ; for sure I am that it is not unknown to you I have already undertaken a work to the same effect, which is in heroical verse, under the title of the *Faerie Queen*, to represent all the moral virtues, assigning to every virtue a knight, to be the patron and defender of the same. . . .' " [1]

In 1584 he had already advanced some way with the work ; and in 1590, going to England with Raleigh, he published the first three books. In 1596 he published three more books, and these, with some stanzas of a seventh book, found after his death, are all that we have of the twelve books originally contemplated. Spenser's epic contains many deep religious truths couched in the form of allegory ; the curious reader of the First Book may see that it contains the germ of the thoughts after-

[1] Croft's *English Literature.*

wards expanded in Bunyan's *Pilgrim's Progress*. Among these may be mentioned the description of Despair and his advice to the Red Cross Knight to commit suicide ; the House of Holiness, where the knight is admitted by the porter Humility, tended by the three maidens, Faith, Hope, and Charity, and comforted by an ancient matron named Mercy. From the top of a hill an old man points out to him a distant view of the heavenly city.

We must not forget the celebrated work that had so great an influence upon the literature of that and the following age, the *Arcadia* of Sir Philip Sidney. That quaint yet poetic, pastoral romance was, in prose, like Spenser's *Faerie Queen* in verse, a treasury of intellectual beauties. It should be remembered in judging the work of Sir Philip Sidney, that he thought very meanly of it himself, and that he never intended it for publication. Dedicating the book to his " Dear lady and fair sister the Countess of Pembroke," he says :—

" You desired me to do it, and your desire, to my heart, is an absolute commandment. Now it is done only for you, only to you."

Aubrey tells us that Sidney

" was wont to take his table-book out of his pocket and write down his notions as they came into his head, as he was hunting on Sarum's pleasant plains."

It was in 1580 that Sidney began the composition of his romance.

A few years since there was exhibited before the Archæological Society at Salisbury a copy of the *Arcadia*, between the leaves of which was found wrapped up the lock of the Queen's hair, and some complimentary lines addressed by Sidney to her. The hair was soft and bright, of a light-brown colour, inclining to red, and on the paper enclosing it was written :—
" This lock of Queen Elizabeth's own hair was presented to Sir Philip Sidney by Her Majesty's owne faire hands, on which he made these verses, and gave them to the Queen on his bended knee, A.D. 1573." And pinned to this was another paper, on which was written in a different hand, supposed to have been Sidney's own, these lines :—

" Her inward worth all outward show transcends,
    Envy her merits with regret commends ;

Like sparkling gems her virtues draw the sight,
And in her conduct she is alwaies bright.
When she imparts her thoughts, her words have
    force,
And sense and wisdom flow in sweet discourse."

Every person remembers his brave words when he had fallen on the field of Zutphen, and while suffering from thirst, a cup of water being presented to him: as his eye met that of a wounded soldier, he exclaimed, pointing to him, "Thy necessity is yet greater than mine."

Well might our great dramatist say of him :—

" His honour stuck upon him as the sun
    In the gray vault of heaven, and by his light
    Did all the chivalry of England move
    To do brave acts ! "

It has been suggested that Sidney's *Arcadia* was modelled upon Sannazzaro's pastoral romance of the same name or title; but it is certain that few works enjoyed so great popularity among scholars as Sidney's, or excited a more controlling influence over the literary taste of its time. Both Cowley and Waller were among its admirers, and it was the solace of the

prison-hours of Charles I. Milton states
that the prayer of Pamela was introduced
into the *Eikon Basilike* from it.

Campbell styled Sidney "warbler of
poetic prose," and we find in addition
some lyric *verse*, scattered on his pages,
that we have been tempted to transcribe.
Take for instance these two stanzas :—

" My true love hath my heart, and I have his,
 By just exchange—one for the other given ;
I hold his dear, and mine he cannot miss ;
 There never was a better bargain driven :—
My true love hath my heart, and I have his.
His heart in me, keeps me and him in one;
 My heart in him his thoughts and senses guides,,
He loves my heart for once it was his own,
 I cherish his because in me it bides ;
My true love hath my heart, and I have his !"

The following leads us from gay to
grave :—

" Since nature's works be good, and death doth
  save
 As nature's work, why should we fear to die ?
Since fear is vain, but when it may preserve,
 Why should we fear that which we cannot fly ?
Fear is more pain than is the pain it fears,—
 Disarming human minds of native might ;
While each conceit an ugly figure bears,
 Which were not ill, well-viewed in reason's
  light."

II.

MORE'S "UTOPIA." — FOX'S "BOOK
OF MARTYRS." — ROGER ASCHAM.—
MONTAIGNE. — BROWNE'S "RELIGIO
MEDICI." — PEPYS'S AND EVELYN'S
"DIARIES."

ONE of the noteworthy books,
known at least to scholars, is
the *Utopia* of Sir Thomas More,
the idea of which was probably taken
mainly from the *Republic* of Plato; at any
rate this is the opinion of Mr. Hallam;
although Sir Thomas was doubtless
familiar with other writers on social and
political economy besides Plato and
Aristotle, for in the famous fragment of
Theopompus of Chios, he might have
found some suggestion. In this writer,
as in Plato, we discover glimpses of a
knowledge of the great Western Continent,
which afterwards reappeared in Pulci,[1]

[1] Adams's *Famous Books.*

and may probably have led, though in-
directly, to the eventual discovery of
America by Columbus. Euhemerus, the
author of *Panchaia*, found his imaginary
commonwealth in a different quarter of
the globe; but it is remarkable that he
places it, as More places his, upon an
island, and in that very Indian Ocean in
which "Utopia" is said to lie. This
famous work seems to have owed its
immediate origin to an embassy in which
More was engaged in 1515.

"He had always been a favourite with
Henry VIII., who, with all his faults, was able
to recognise merit when he saw it; and while at
Antwerp, More met one Peter Giles, a man of
renown; between them an intimate friendship was
soon formed. It was there and then that Sir
Thomas wrote the second book of his *Utopia*, the
first having been composed at London the year
preceding. The manuscript having been read by
Erasmus, was forthwith published in Latin, and
'saluted on all sides by a chorus of decided
admiration.'"

And many translations of the work have
since been published.

Following the chronological order, we
meet with the well-known *Book of Martyrs*,

by John Fox, who, espousing the Protestant faith, shared with many others of
his creed the persecutions then incident
thereto.

" From the time of his expulsion from his college
at Oxford until his death, the career of Fox was
marked by a series of misfortunes which probably
assisted him in sympathising with the sufferings of
those martyrs whose trials he was so soon to put
on record, and whose example, so far as it taught
him patience in tribulation, he faithfully followed."

Now that he was deprived of his
academic emoluments, he had to seek
assistance from his Protestant friends, and
after enduring many trials and adversities,
he went with others to their asylum at
Antwerp, and then settled at Basle, where
he devoted himself to the great history
with which his name is associated, and
which took eleven years to complete.
He here found employment chiefly in
revising manuscripts, which proved adequate to his support. After the accession
of Elizabeth to the throne, Fox returned
to London, and we find him living in the
memorable Grub Street,—

"then, as in the days of Pope, the asylum of
the more laborious but less affluent authors ; and

from that time until his death in 1587 he was occupied in literary work for John Day, the printer."

When his Martyrology was begun is not ascertained, but it is supposed that the idea of its compilation may have first occurred to him while engaged in studying the history of the Church at college; although it has been stated that it was first suggested to Fox by Lady Jane Grey. When it is remembered that his work was written in Latin, the translation of which forms three huge folio volumes, we can form some estimate of the enormous labour he had devoted to it. It is satisfactory to learn that the publication of this book was an immediate and signal success, for

" he received the cordial approbation of the heads of the Church, and the ' Acts and Monuments ' were ordered to be set up in every one of the parish churches of England," etc.

How greatly this important protest against spiritual despotism has contributed to the onward march of human progress and civil and religious freedom it would be impossible to estimate. It was this book, accompanied with the Bible, that gave inspiration to Bunyan, and stirred his wonderful zeal and energy to pourtray for the world his immortal allegory, *The Pilgrim's Progress.*

We now introduce a different type of student life, Roger Ascham, who is known to us by his quaint work entitled *Toxophilus, or the Schole of Shootinge,* and who but for his love of archery would not probably have written *The Schoolmaster,* or if the exigencies of his profession had not convinced him that the mode of education common in his time was not the best that it was possible to devise. It is only too clear that the literary outcome of a man is inevitably affected by even the minute incidents of his career, and, therefore, had we space it would be interesting to summarise the life of this noteworthy writer. But it must suffice to state that he was moved to the compiling his *Toxophilus,* to cite his antique style,

"Partlye provoked by the counsell of some gentlemen, partlye moved by the love whiche I have alwayes borne toward shotynge, I have written this lytle treatise, wherein if I have not satisfied any man, I trust he wyll the rather be content with my doying, because I am (I suppose)

the firste whiche hath sayde any thynge in this matter."

It may be stated that *The Schole of Shootinge* is in two parts, and in the form of a conversation between two college fellows—"Toxophilus" (the lover of archery) and " Philologus" (the lover o learning)—who hold colloquy amid the woods and fields near Cambridge, con-' cerning the respective claims of the *Booke* and the *Bowe.* He became prebend in York Cathedral, and he died in 1568, greatly lamented by the Queen, who, it is said, exclaimed, " I would rather have lost ten thousand pounds than to have lost my old tutor, Ascham ! " Shortly after his death his larger and most celebrated work, *The Schoolmaster*, was published. In his preface, the author informs the reader as to the origin of the work ; which appears to have arisen out of a dinner given by Sir William Cecil.

"At which were present the most of her Majesties most honorable privye counsell, and the rest serving in verye good place. I was glad to be there in the companie of so many wise and good men together, as hardly could have been picked out againe, out of alle England beside."

It seems that one of this illustrious company referred to the condition of Eton College, and the .system of tuition then existing, being accompanied with harshness in discipline, etc. This incident seems to have aroused Ascham, and induced him to prepare his treatise on the subject of education. His favourite pupil was the gentle and accomplished but ill-fated Lady Jane Grey.

Montaigne, the essayist (*temp.* 1533 to 1592), whose name was derived from the chateau where he was born and resided, gives us no definite idea of what induced him to write his famous essays, which grew into existence during a period of ten years,—garrulous as he is on a variety of subjects. It is very probable that if they were at first intended to have any special form at all, it was that of a table-book or journal; such books were never more commonly kept than in the sixteenth century. But the author must have been more or less conscious of an order existing in the seeming disorder of his thoughts, since he has arranged them into chapters. Although this rambling essayist has made titles to his chapters, he is so discursive that his digressions prevail more frequently than any direct line of thought ; and his quotations are more conspicuous still in his motley pages. His sole object, he admits,[1] was to leave for his relatives and friends a mental portrait of himself, defects and all ; while he professed indifference alike as to his fame, or the utility of his writings. Yet notwithstanding all this, his *Essays* have ever been found among the accepted literature of the

[1] Montaigne, in his preface to his *Essays*, thus writes :—" Here, reader, is a book written in all good faith. It warns thee at the outset, that I have proposed to myself no end but a family and private one ; I had in it no thought of the profit or of my own glory ; my powers are not capable of such an undertaking. I have dedicated it to the special convenience of my relations and friends, in order that when they have lost me (which they must needs do very soon), they may here recover some traits of my character and humour, and that by this means they may preserve more perfect and lively the knowledge which they had of me in life." His two first books of *Essays* were given to the press in 1580 at Bordeaux. He had begun their composition at least eight years before ; it was slowly and by degrees that they took shape under his hand ; and he kept continually adding to them, as he admits.

library. Montaigne seems to have lived a life of elegant leisure, and delighted in literary and scholastic pursuits. In his study, which he has minutely described, he read and wrote, and indulged himself in the luxury of studious retirement. As to the influence his productions have exerted in the world of letters, we endorse the estimate of an able critic,[1] who remarks :—

" It would be impossible for the stoutest defender of the importance of form in literature, to assign the chief part in Montaigne's influence to style. It is the method, or rather the manner, of thinking of which that style is the garment, which has in reality exercised an influence over the world. Like all writers, except Shakespeare, Montaigne thoroughly and completely exhibits the intellectual and moral complexion of his own time."

Another work well known to the studious reader is the *Religio Medici* of Sir Thomas Browne, who took his degree as Doctor of Medicine in 1634, and shortly after took up his abode at Shipden Hall, near Halifax, where he composed his quaint and picturesque book.

[1] Mr. Saintsbury, *Encyclopædia Britannica.*

" There seems no sufficient reason to question Browne's declaration that this piece was composed for his private exercise and satisfaction, and not intended for publication."

Dr. Johnson leans to this opinion also ; he says :—

" This has, perhaps, sometimes befallen others, and this, I am willing to believe, did really happen to Dr. Browne ; but there is surely some reason to doubt the truth of the complaint so frequently made of surreptitious editions."

Yet, on the other hand, in his address to the reader, prefixed to the first authorised edition, Sir Thomas says :—

" This, I confess, about seven years past, with some others of affinity thereto, for my private exercise and satisfaction, I had at leisurable hours composed ; which being communicated unto one, it became common unto many, and was by transcription successively corrupted, until it arrived in a most depraved copy at the press. He that shall peruse that work, and shall take notice of sundry particulars and personal expressions therein, will easily discern the intention was not public."

As a brief example of his style, we cite the following from his *Religio Medici*, in which he treats of God in nature :—

" There are two books from whence I collect my divinity ; besides that written one of God, one of His servant, Nature,—that universal and public manuscript, that lies expanded unto the eyes of all. Those that never see Him in the one have discovered Him in the other : this was the Scripture and theology of the heathen ; the natural motions of the sun made them more admire Him, than its supernatural station did the children of Israel. Surely the heathen knew better how to join and read these mystical letters, than we Christians, who cast a more careless eye on these common hieroglyphics, and disdain to suck Divinity from the flowers of nature. . . . I call the effects of nature the works of God, Whose hand and instrument she only is; to ascribe His actions unto her, is to devolve the honour of the agent upon the instrument."

We subjoin another extract, which is characteristic of his style :—

"Time past is gone like a shadow : make times to come, present ; conceive that near, which may be far off. Approximate thy latter times by present appearances of them ; be like a neighbour unto death, and think there is little to come : and since there is something in us that must live on, join both lives together, unite them in thy thoughts and actions, and live in one but for the other. He Who thus ordereth the purposes of this life, will never be far from the next, and is in some manner already in it, by a happy conformity and close apprehension of it."

The *Religio Medici* was composed at
leisure hours, and, as it appears, never
would have reached the public, but for the
necessity of the author justifying himself
from the charge of responsibility for the
corrupt piracies which got into print from
privately circulated copies of his MS. Besides the piratical editions, during the
author's lifetime eight authorized editions
were published; and besides these the
work was translated into many European
languages.

There is always a charm about auto-
biographical books, even if—as in the
instance of Pepys's *Diary*—its literature
be not of the highest order. This work,
however, possessed a twofold attraction.
To those who like gossip about the
personal details of the writer, as well as
to others who prefer historic incidents
given by an eyewitness, Pepys will
prove, although an egotistical, yet a
pleasant companion. It is not my purpose to sketch this worthy, he himself
having rendered that service unnecessary;
and it will suffice to mention the date when
he began to keep his *Diary*, which was

January 1st, 1659-60, to the end of May 1669, when he was obliged, from defective vision, to discontinue his daily task. In his last entry he says :—

"Thus ends all that I doubt I shall be ever able to do with my own eyes in the keeping of my journal ; and, therefore, whatever comes of it I must forbear, and therefore resolve, from this time forward, to have it kept by my people in longhand, and must be content to set down no more than is fit for them and all the world to know."

That his *Diary* was originally written in shorthand was not without cause, since when it was deciphered and published in 1825, the editor intimated that it had been found " absolutely necessary" to make numerous curtailments.

As a picture of the times in which he lived, it is a valuable work, and although not equal to Evelyn's *Diary*, is yet very amusing for the details it gives of characters and events of that epoch.

There is a wonderful freshness about this work, as if it were of yesterday, rather than two centuries old; and in this fact lies its chief charm. It differs from ordinary books of its class in this, that—

" the author's thoughts, instead of having been
written out in the usual way, seem to have recorded
themselves by some involuntary automatic process,
as words are registered and preserved by the
phonograph. By this means the idiosyncrasies
of the bustling, patriotic, money-making secretary
have been kept in their original freshness for the
entertainment of the present generation." [1]

One of the " healthiest and most in-
structive of books" is the *Diary of John
Evelyn*, although it does not, in all
respects, strictly fulfil what the term im-
plies. Evelyn's *Diary* was found, among
other papers, at his country seat at Wotton,
in Surrey. Evelyn has himself told us in
what way the book originated :—

" In imitation of what I had seen my father
do," he remarks, when speaking of himself in his
twelfth year, " I began to observe matters more
punctually, which I did use to set down in a blank
almanack."

These fragmentary memoranda were,
it seems, transferred from the blank
almanacs to the quarto blank book in
which they were afterwards found, and
from which the work was printed. This
quarto volume, still at Wotton, consists

[1] E. S. Fisher.

of seven hundred pages, written closely by Evelyn, in a very small hand, and comprising the continuous records of fifty-six years,—a period the most romantic and stirring in the English annals. Sir Walter Scott said that "he had never seen a mine so rich." And of Evelyn himself, it may be said that he was one of the noblest and most exemplary of men in an age not remarkable for purity and virtue in its high places of power.

The manuscript diary of the celebrated John Evelyn lay among the family papers, at his country seat, from the period of his death, in 1706, until their rare interest and value were discovered in the following singular manner.

Mr. Upcott, of the London Institution, was requested to arrange and catalogue the library at Wotton, and one day Lady Evelyn remarked, as he had expressed his great interest in the collection of autographs, the manuscript of Evelyn's *Sylva* would be interesting to him. Replying, as may be imagined, in the affirmative, the servant was directed to bring the papers from a loft in the old mansion, and soon Upcott had the delight of finding among the collection the manuscript *Diary of John Evelyn,*—one of the most finished specimens of autobiography in the whole realm of English literature.   The work was published in 1818.   Wotton House is embosomed among the grand old forest trees of his estate, and these he described in his *Sylva,* during his lifetime.

III.

Feltham's "Resolves."—"Emblems."—Ballads.—"Robin Hood."—"King Arthur."—Shakespeare.—Hobbes of Malmesbury.—St. Pierre.—"Baron Munchausen."—Bunyan's "Pilgrim's Progress."—Dryden.—Pope.—"Robinson Crusoe."—"Gulliver's Travels."—Walton's "Angler."—White's "Selborne."

IT is well for us occasionally to turn aside from the thronged thoroughfares of busy life, and escaping from its turmoil and strife of tongues, in the cool eventide to con over some of the suggestive and sagacious tomes of the olden times. When these volumes were written, "the hum of Babel did not reach the scholar's hermitage," for it was then a time of quiet meditation, as ours is of unrest and earnest activity. One of

these philosophic thinkers—Owen Feltham—thus quaintly writes in one of his
letters :—

"I have lived in such a course as that my
books have ever been my delight and recreation;
and that which some call idleness, I will call the
sweetest part of my life, and that is my thinking."

His well-known book of aphorisms,
which he called *Resolves*, like Arthur War-
wick's *Spare Minutes*, a contemporary work,
is replete with sententious wisdom. But
perhaps more prominent among these
magnates of the seventeenth century was
Thomas Fuller. A man of multifarious
learning and great judgment, he combined
within himself those qualities which minister to entertainment as well as instruction
in an eminent degree.

"Next to Shakespeare," said Coleridge, "I am
not certain whether Thomas Fuller, beyond all
other writers, does not excite in me the sense and
emotion of the marvellous. He was incomparably
the most sensible and least prejudiced great man of
an age that boasted of a galaxy of great men."

His memory was wonderful, and for
quaintness and humour he has been compared to "Hudibrastic" Butler. To the

noble order of pioneers and martyrs for civic and religious liberty—the fraternity of Cromwell, Hampden, Pym, and Milton— we are indebted for some of the noblest inspirations in verse and prose which stir the common heart of humanity to this day.

" It was the short and splendid period of Puritan mastery interpolated between the Shakespeare of Elizabeth and the Dryden of Charles II. ; and a crowd of cavalier poets before the Revolution and after the Restoration. Side by side with these, ' with his garland and singing robes about him,' stands the solitary sublime form of John Milton, perhaps the very noblest of England's sons." [1]

These are the great masters of the lyre and the pen, who have stood for the defence of human rights, both civil and religious ; and who have also, in melodious verse and eloquent prose, taught us the high themes of Christian philosophy and the practical ethics of daily life. What a brilliant constellation of stars of the first magnitude then shone forth on the literary firmament,—Bacon, Shakespeare, Milton, Cromwell, Bunyan, and Jeremy Taylor, Barrow, Hall, South, Leighton, and Hooke.

[1] Canon Farrar.

They lived, although in troublous times,
calm and elevated lives, and knew by personal experience the import of the beautiful remark of Norris of Bemerton, that

" when all is still and quiet in a man, then will
God speak to him, in the cool of the day ; and in
that calm and silence of the passions, the Divine
Voice will be heard."

These worthies lived for a high purpose,
and they have bequeathed to us the fruit-
age of their meditative thoughts. Said
one of their number :—

" Intellectual pleasures are of a nobler kind than
any others ; they are the inclinations of Heaven,
and the entertainments of the Deity."

Francis Quarles is only known to the
general reader by his *Emblems*, which first
appeared in 1635. During the middle ages
there were several writers of this order, for
George Wither compiled *A Collection of
Emblems, Ancient and Modern*, etc. But
the fame of Quarles exceeds all others in
this class of literature.

" His visible poetry," said Fuller, " (I mean his
Emblems), is excellent, catching therein the eye
and fancy at one draught."

Quarles wrote in and for a rude age, and

consequently, as the popular taste has changed since then, much that was acceptable to his is less adapted to our day; however much some persons may admire his antique style of illustrating moral and religious truth. Without impugning his undoubted piety, he seems to have indulged his wayward fancy with incongruous oddities,—or strangely "endeavoured to mix the waters of Helicon with those of Zion;" and these eccentricities are unfortunately more conspicuous than are his higher qualities as a writer. He seems, moreover, to have written his verse to suit the grotesque wood-cut illustrations of the book. These *Emblems* were written, it is believed, at the suggestion of his friend Benlowes, author of *Theophila*, whom Pope describes as "propitious to block-heads," and of whom Warburton said that he was "famous for his own bad poetry and for patronising bad poets." Quarles made an excellent little volume, to which he gave the name *Enchiridion*,—a book of aphorisms and quaint epigrammatical apothegms. It is as a prose writer that we discover his excellence.

A brief reference to one or two of our most noted old English ballads seems to lie within the range of our investigations. Perhaps the best known of these are *King Arthur and his Knights of the Round Table*, and *Robin Hood*. Longfellow calls the ballads " the gipsy children of song, born under green hedgerows in the leafy lanes and by-paths of literature in the genial summer time." The troubadours of Provence were of the class; and in England, Drayton wrote the stirring ballad of *Agincourt;* and in the same sixteenth century probably was written the *Nut-brown Maid.*

An annotated edition of Bishop Percy's well-known *Reliques of Ancient English Poetry*, edited by Mr. H. B. Wheatley, has imparted to this subject an increased interest, it having made available some new information concerning the original manuscript source of these antique ballads. The manuscript itself is about fifteen inches in length by five wide; some of its pages at beginning and end are lost, having been " used," it is stated, " by some servants to light the fire." The

handwriting of it is assigned to the year
1650. This precious relic was found by
Percy under a bureau in the house of his
friend Humphrey Pitt, of Shiffnal, Shrop-
shire. The reticence which Percy and his
friends observed respecting this manuscript, and their refusal to permit any
person to examine it, made it a matter
of doubt as to whether Percy's claim
of his ballads being founded upon it
was valid. Ritson the antiquary, and
others, made common cause against the
Bishop; and yet he kept his secret
till his death. But thanks to the enthusiastic devotion of Dr. Furnivall, the long-
coveted relic has been given to the world,
in the year of grace 1868, now rescued
from the risks and perils to which, in the
manuscript form, it has been so long exposed. Bishop Percy's *Reliques of Ancient
English Poetry* appeared in 1765. This
famous work, consisting of old heroic
ballads and songs, was chiefly derived
from the old folio manuscript, with the
addition of some pieces from the Pepys
collection at Cambridge, the Ashmolean
library at Oxford, the British Museum,

and the works of our earlier poets.
The collection has always been considered of great value to our literature,
for its reproducing the old chivalry and
minstrelsy of Elizabethan times. This
work it was that captivated Scott, and
inspired his *Minstrelsy of the Scottish
Border.*

The *Robin Hood* legend dates about the
close of the twelfth century. The traditions concerning this English outlaw are
mostly derived from Stow's *Chronicle ;*
but modern research has tended very
much to the belief that Robin Hood's
existence is merely one of the myths of the
middle ages. The famous ballad is, however, one of the most popular, not only with
the poets, but the public generally. Stow
tells us :—

"In the reign of Richard I. (1190) were
manie robbers and outlawes, among which Robin
Hood and Little John, renowned thieves, continued
in the woodes, despoyling and robbing the goodes
of the rich. The said Robin entertained an hundred tall men and good archers, with such spoyles
and thefts as he got, upon whom four hundred (were
they never so strong) durst not give the onset.
Poore men's goodes he spared, abundantlie reliev-

ing them with that which by theft he got from the abbeys and the houses of rich old carles; whom Maior (the historian) blameth for his rapine and theft, but of all the thieves he affirmeth him to be the prince and the most gentle thiefe."

The Robin Hood ballads were, doubtless, the popular protest against the oppression of the privileged classes, uttered in song; and as such they may be regarded as the prophecy of the better times that followed.

Now as to that pet legend of the poets, Prince Arthur with his Knights of the Round Table, he is supposed by some to have been identical with an actual Sovereign in England, in the sixth century. The Welsh bards refer to a Prince Arthur fighting against the Saxons; and upon this basis the Arthur of romance is believed to have had a real existence. The Arthur of the famous legend was, by the enchantments of the sage Merlin, enabled to do many wonderful things, and ultimately to assume the crown of England, and also to marry " the fairest woman in the land." With her, as a part of her dower, he acquired the enchanted " round table," which had once belonged to her father. About this he formed the famous circle of " Knights ; " with these he began to hold his brilliant court at Winchester, the wonderful series of exploits at home and abroad, and the countless adventures recorded in the veritable chronicle of Geoffrey of Monmouth. Even in his day,—that is, in the twelfth century,—this romantic legend had become incorporated with much of our poetic literature, nor has it ceased to fascinate the minstrels even to this day.

Of the dramas of Shakespeare—who has been styled "the protagonist on the great arena of modern poetry, and the glory of the human intellect"—it seems almost superfluous to speak, so much has already been written. Owing to the para-lysing influences of the civil war which followed some score of years after the first collective edition of his works, it was reserved for more recent times to discover the opulence of his wonderful genius. Nor is it necessary to remind the reader of the innumerable editions which have appeared during the century. It is well known to every student, that many if not most of his historical dramas have their prototype in some of the old chroniclers ; for instance, numerous parallels as to names, characters, and incidents exist in *Macbeth, Henry VIII.*, and other plays which are mainly identical with those in Holinshed.

Romeo and Juliet, a story which the Veronese believe to be historically true, in the hands of Shakespeare has become the love story of the world. It has been traced back to 1303, as a ballad ; and some two centuries later, Massaccio, a Neapolitan, gave embodiment to the story in a romance, changing the scene to Sienna, and varying the catastrophe.

Aubrey, the antiquary, informs us that our great dramatist took the humour of Dogberry, in *Much Ado about Nothing*, from an actual occurrence which happened at Grendon, in Buckinghamshire, during one of the poet's journeys between Stratford and London, and that the constable was living at Grendon when Aubrey first went to Oxford, about the year 1642.

The old chroniclers Roger of Wendover and Matthew Paris give the earliest traditions of the *Wandering Jew.* According to Menzel, the story is but an allegory symbolizing heathenism. Lacroix suggests that it represents the Hebrew race,—dispersed and wandering through the world, but not destroyed.

Next to Bacon, the most conspicuous name in philosophy of his time is that of Thomas Hobbes, of Malmesbury. His renowned work, *The Leviathan*, was published in 1651; and although he is certainly of the school of the French Freethinkers, if not Atheists, yet his rhetoric is so clear, nervous, and forcible, that his work is believed to have exerted a controlling influence upon human opinion at the time. He is amenable to critical and correct taste, as well as to morals, for his opinions, which few in our day would be found willing to espouse. It is said that Hobbes was fond of long walks, and that he carried in the head of his cane a pen and ink-horn, as well as a note-book in his pocket; so that he was at any moment able to commit his thoughts and opinions to paper, as they occurred to him ; and thus he formed his *Leviathan*.

It is generally supposed that St. Pierre's *Paul and Virginia* is a purely fictitious narrative ; but this is not so, the general outline of the story being drawn from facts. The old church of Pamplemousses withstands the ravages of time, and the Morne de la Découverte will be a more enduring monument than all. The memory of *Paul and Virginia* is still cherished by the people, many of whom bear their names.

Paul and Virginia, although the production of a French author, is so universally known in the translation as a choice little romantic idyl, that it well deserves a place of honour. St. Pierre, its author, like our Goldsmith, seems to have been a hapless son of genius, for he wrote his immortal tale in a garret on the Rue St. Etienne-du-Mont, Paris. A touching incident connected with the manuscript of *Paul and Virginia* is recorded by L. Aimé Martin. Madame Necker invited St. Pierre to bring his new story into her salon, and read it

before publication to a company of distinguished and enlightened auditors.
She promised that the judges she would
convene to hear him were among those
she esteemed most worthy. Monsieur
Necker himself, as a distinguished favour,
would be at home on the occasion.
Buffon, the Abbé Galiani, and M. Ger-
main were among the tribunal when
St. Pierre appeared and sat down with
the manuscript open before him. At
first he was heard in profound silence;
he went on, and the attention grew
languid, the august assembly began to
whisper, to yawn, and then listen no
longer. M. de Buffon pulled out his
watch, and called for his horses; those
sitting near the door noiselessly slipped
out; one of the company was seen in
profound slumber; some of the ladies
wept, but Monsieur Necker jeered at
them, and they, ashamed of their tears,
dared not confess how much interested
they had been. When the reading was
finished, not a word of praise was uttered.
Madame Necker criticised the conver-
sations in the book, and spoke of the

tedious and commonplace action in the story. A shower of iced-water seemed to fall on poor St. Pierre, who retired from the room in a state of overwhelming depression. He felt as if a sentence of death had been pronounced on his story, and that *Paul and Virginia* was unworthy to appear before the public eye. But a man of genius, Joseph Vernet, the artist, who had not been present at the reading at Madame Necker's, dropped in one morning on St. Pierre in his garret, and revived his almost sinking courage. " Perhaps St. Pierre will read his new story to his friend Vernet," he said. So the author took up his manuscript again, which had been since the fatal day laid aside, and began to read. As Vernet listened, the charm fell upon him, and at every page he uttered an exclamation of delight. Soon he ceased to praise, he only wept; and when the author reached that part of the book which Madame Necker had found so much fault with, St. Pierre proposed to omit that part of the narrative; but Vernet would not consent to omit anything. "My friend," exclaimed Vernet, "you are a great painter, and I dare to promise you a splendid reputation." His prophecy was speedily verified, for within the year fifty editions of *Paul and Virginia* are said to have been published.

The authorship of the *Travels of Baron Munchausen* was some time a secret; but the book is now ascertained to have been by Rodolph Eric Raspe, a scientific German, who died in 1794, while superintending some mining operations at Mucress, in the south of Ireland. While employed in the mining districts of Cornwall, he wrote his *Travels of Baron Munchausen.* He is believed to have been the original of the character of Dousterswivel, which Scott introduced into the *Antiquary.*

The Pilgrim's Progress was written while Bunyan was in prison at Bedford, and but half conscious of the gifts which he possessed. It was written for his own entertainment, and therefore without the thought—so fatal in its effects, and so hard to be resisted— of what the world would say about it.

It was written in compulsory quiet, when he was comparatively unexcited by the effort of perpetual preaching, and the shapes of things could present themselves to him as they really were. *The Pilgrim's Progress* is a book which when once read can never be forgotten ; it is, and will remain, unique of its kind,—an imperishable monument of the form in which the problem of life presented itself to a person of singular truthfulness, simplicity, and piety, who, after many struggles, accepted the Puritan creed as the adequate solution of it.

It may not be generally known that there exist in the British Museum the manuscripts, and also a printed copy of a work, written by Guillaume de Guileville, a prior of Calais, who died in 1360. This work, both as to its plan and its characters, bears a remarkable resemblance to the allegory of Bunyan ; and it has been supposed that that work may have suggested to him the design for his *Pilgrim's Progress.* The work of Guileville was an allegoric poem written in French, but translated, and familiar, therefore, to the English public. Yet it must be remembered that Bunyan was an unlettered man, and, as far as known, possessed only his Bible and Fox's *Book of Martyrs;* might he not have been wholly ignorant of the existence of the work in question, and the similarity of its plan with that of the *Pilgrim's Progress* have been an accidental coincidence?

His knowledge of books must have been very small, but the English version of the Bible, in which our language exhibits its highest force and perfection, had been studied by him so intensely, that he was completely saturated with its spirit.

"He wrote unconsciously in its style, and the innumerable Scripture quotations with which his works are incrusted, like a mosaic, harmonize without any incongruity with the general tissue of his language."

Bunyan's natural temperament was sensitive to an unusual degree. To his fertile brain images crowded quickly upon him, and his ready wit as quickly caught the 'points of similarity between

5

the various stages of Christian experience
in this world and his allegory. No one
seems to have helped him in the composition of the work. Like Milton in his
blindness, Bunyan in his imprisonment
had his spiritual perception made all the
brighter by his exclusion from the glare
of the outside world. Many persons
who may be conversant with the *Pilgrim's
Progress* may not fully appreciate how
much of fervent piety and strong sense
as well as picturesque imagery abound
in his numerous productions, which are
said to amount to the number of the
years of his life,—sixty. Dean Stanley
has justly remarked that—

"We all need to be cheered by the help of .
Greatheart and Standfast, and Valiant-for-the-
Truth and good old Honesty! Some of us have
been in Doubting Castle, some in the Slough of
Despond. Some have experienced the tempta-
tions of Vanity Fair ; all of us have to climb
the Hill of Difficulty ; all of us need to be instructed by the Interpreter in the House Beautiful ;
all of us bear the same burden ; all of us need the
same armour in our fight with Apollyon ; all of us
have to pass through the Wicket-gate,—to pass
through the dark river ; and for all of us (if God
so will) there wait the shining ones at the gates

of the Celestial City ! Who does not love to linger over the life story of the 'immortal dreamer,' as one of those characters for whom man has done so little, and God so much ! "

Dryden's celebrated ode for the festival of St. Cecilia's Day is considered one of the best illustrations of the pliancy of our English extant. One day Lord Boling-broke chanced to call on Dryden, whom he found in unusual agitation, and on inquiring the cause he replied :—

"I have been up all night ; my musical friends made me promise to write them an ode for the feast of St. Cecilia, and I have been so struck with the subject which occurred to me that I could not leave it till I had completed it ; here it is finished at one sitting."

The poem is designed to exhibit the different passions excited by Timotheus in the mind of Alexander, feasting a triumph-ant conqueror in Persepolis. Dryden wrote this grand ode at Burleigh House, where his translation of *Virgil* was partly executed. This ode has been pronounced unequalled by anything of its kind since classic times.

If Dryden is to be considered a master

in lyric, Pope may be called the most attractive of didactic poets. Yet the latter confessed that Dryden's productions first inspired him with the love of the muse.

Pope devoted five years to his translation of *Homer*, and it proved a great pecuniary as well as literary success. The manuscript of his version of Homer's *Iliad*, now in the British Museum, presents a curious illustration of the title once conferred upon the author, of " paper-sparing Pope," as the writing is upon the backs and corners of old letters and fragments and scraps of paper. His *Essay on Criticism* was, on its appearance, highly praised by Addison in the *Spectator*, which gave it at once great success.

The *Rape of the Lock*, which Johnson styles " the most airy, ingenious, and delightful of all Pope's compositions," was occasioned by a frolic of gallantry. Pope says in his dedication to Arabella Fermor :—

" It was intended only to divert a few young ladies who have good sense and good humour enough to laugh, not only at their sex's little unguarded follies, but at their own. But as it was communicated with the air of a secret, it soon found its way into the world. An imperfect copy having been offered to a bookseller, you had the good nature, for my sake, to consent to the publication of one more correct. . . . As to the following cantos, all the passages of them are as fabulous as the vision at the beginning, or the transformation at the end (except the loss of your hair, which I always mention with reverence)."

Pope sought the solace of the muse to beguile his hours of physical suffering. At the age of sixteen he wrote his *Pastorals*, and soon afterwards his poems *The Messiah* and *Essay on Criticism*. Pope's bodily infirmity caused him to be at times very irascible, which once occasioned his long-tried friend, Bishop Atterbury, in pleasantry to characterise him as *Mens curva in corpore curva*. His *Essay on Man*, which was his next production in order of time, so replete with nervous and picturesque passages, is yet tinctured with the heresies of his friend Lord Bolingbroke.

Dr. Johnson, referring to the *Essay on Man*, after saying that Bolingbroke supplied the poet with the principles of the essay, adds, "These principles it is not my business to clear from obscurity, dogmatism, or falsehood."

The *Dunciad* was inscribed to Boling-broke, to whose suggestion he was indebted for the idea and many of the principles which are therein espoused. It was not until the fourth and last book was pub-lished that Pope avowed himself to be the author, the earlier portions being issued anonymously, for fear that those writers he had attacked would retort upon him.

Defoe's *Robinson Crusoe*, when first published, and for some time afterwards, was considered as a genuine history; and even since it has been found to be ficti-tious few books have equalled it in popu-larity. Its merits have been disparaged on account of its want of originality;

"but really," says Sir Walter Scott, "the story of Selkirk, which had been published a few years before, appears to have furnished our author with so little beyond the bare idea of a man living on an uninhabited island, that it seems quite imma-terial whether he took his hint from that or any other similar story."

Sutcliffe, in his history of the island of

Juan Fernandez, from its discovery in 1572, gave to his volume the title of *Crusoniana*, from the fact that it was the well-known abode of Alexander Selkirk on this island which furnished Defoe with the materials of his inimitable romance of *Robinson Crusoe.* From this source it is known that there was, previously to Alexander Selkirk, a solitary tenant of the island, whose sojourn there, as recorded by Dampier and Ringrose, must have been known to Defoe, and to the same source may be traced the original of the story of " Man Friday " and his discovery of his father in *Robinson Crusoe.* The following is the extract referring to it :—

" At the moment of the hurried escape of a crew of buccaneers from Juan Fernandez, one of the crew, a Mosquito Indian named William, happened to be in the woods adjacent hunting goats, so that the ship was under sail before he got back to the bay. Poor Will had only the clothes on his back, a knife, a gun, and a small horn of powder with a few shot. His situation became still more critical when the Spaniards entered the bay, and having caught sight of him made a diligent search; but he eluded their pursuit, and remained the sole occupant of the island. His personal history, as given by

Dampier, is almost as romantic as that of Robinson Crusoe."

It was in 1719 that this immortal book made its appeal to the public, but not until it had been rejected by nearly the whole fraternity of London publishers, which is not saying much for their critical acumen. William Taylor, more astute, is said to have cleared a thousand pounds by his publication of the book, which rose into immediate popularity. The place where Defoe composed his romance is believed to have been Stoke Newington, where he was living at that time in retirement. This is the work upon which the fame of this voluminous writer depends. It has been translated and published in almost every written anguage, and still enjoys literally a world-wide renown.

Swift's *Gulliver's Travels* was published without the name of the author; but it was soon discovered, for it was at once greeted with applause. Johnson said of the work that it was

"so new and strange that it filled the reader with a mingled emotion of merriment and amazement. It was read with such avidity that the

price of the first edition was raised before the
second could be made ; it was read by the high
and the low, the learned and the illiterate.   Criticism was for awhile lost in wonder : no rules of
judgment were applied to a book written in open
defiance of truth and regularity."

As a wonderful satire upon the follies
and excesses of those times, as well as an
extravaganza for amusement, the book is
yet well known.

This famous politico-satirical romance is
one of his works still in vogue, and the
work upon which his reputation as a prose
writer was established.   Swift's personal
history is in itself a romance; indeed, it
seems to have been tinted with insanity,
but it is not our province to refer to
this.

Of Isaac Walton's *Complete Angler* so
much has been written that one would
think no more need be added.   Charles
Lamb said, "It might sweeten a man's
temper at any time to read it ; " and
a later authority says, "To speak of
Walton is to fall to praising him ; " but
Byron, who was no angler, thus refers to
him :—

" Angling, too, that solitary vice,
  Whatever Isaac Walton sings or says ;
  The quaint, old, cruel coxcomb, in his gullet
  Should have a hook, and a small trout to pull it."

But people in the seventeenth century concerned themselves little or nothing with animal suffering. The advice which Walton gives for the treatment of live-bait is proof sufficient. *The Complete Angler* is Walton's true title to fame. It was published in 1653, the year in which Oliver Cromwell was declared Protector, and Walton lived to see his work pass through several editions. It has long since taken an undisputed place among English classics; while to speak of its poetry, wisdom, and piety would be to repeat criticism which has passed into commonplace.

All we can learn about the origin of the work is from the author's preface, where he quaintly says :—

"I think fit to tell thee these following truths : that I did neither undertake, nor write, nor publish, and much less own, this discourse to please myself ; and having been too easily drawn to do all to please others, as I propose not the gaining of credit by this undertaking, so I would not

willingly lose any part of that to which I had a just
title before I began it, and do therefore desire and
hope, if I deserve not commendations, yet I may
obtain pardon. And though this discourse may be
liable to some exceptions, yet I cannot doubt but
that most readers may receive so much pleasure or
profit by it as may make it worthy the time of their
perusal, if they be not too grave or busy men.
And this is all the confidence that I can put on
concerning the merit of what is here offered to
their consideration and censure ; and if the last
prove too severe, as I have a liberty, so I am
resolved to use it, and neglect all sour censures.
And I wish the reader also to take notice that in
writing of it I have made myself a recreation of a
recreation ; and that it might prove so to him, and
not read dull and tediously, I have in several places
mixed, not any scurrility, but some innocent, harmless mirth, of which, if thou be a severe, sour-com-
plexioned man, then I here disallow thee to be a
competent judge; for divines say, there are *offences
given, and offences not given, but taken.*

" And I am the willinger to justify the pleasant
part of it because, though it is known I can be
serious at seasonable times, yet the whole discourse
is, or rather was, a picture of my own disposition,
especially in such days and times as I have laid
aside business and gone a fishing with honest Nat
and R. Roe ; but they are gone, and with them
most of my pleasant hours, even as a shadow that
passeth away and returns not."

" Who ever read Gilbert White's *Natural*

History of Selborne without the most exquisite delight?" was asked by a writer in
Blackwood's Magazine. White's *Natural
History of Selborne* and Walton's *Complete
Angler* are both books possessing such
singular attraction to contemplative readers
that their popularity has ever continued
to increase. The cause of the esteem in
which they both are held is mainly the
same.

"Honest, manly, and godly in their tone, simple
and clear in their style, with no ostentation, clearness and accuracy of observation in those subjects
which each particularly affected, and with the
charm of enthusiasm, they are models for all succeeding writers on kindred subjects."

Gilbert White, the author, seems to have
resembled Isaac Walton in his love of rural
sights and sounds—the one choosing the
woods and the other the streams. The
lack of systematic arrangement of his
letters, as well as the tone of the letters
themselves, render it probable that they
were originally written without any design
of publication. This was his only book,
moreover, and this is suggestive of his
freedom from literary ambition. His

letters give us not only, as a naturalist, much interesting information, but they also afford us a better idea of the author's personal life and character than is elsewhere supplied.

IV.

MILTON.—YOUNG'S "NIGHT THOUGHTS."
—DR. JOHNSON.—GRAY.—CAMPBELL.

"NEVER does poetry better attain its true dignity than when it aspires to lay its choicest garlands at the feet of Him for Whom earth had no crown save one of thorns." The words of Milton are as true as they are eloquent, when he declares the proper office of the poet to be "to celebrate in glorious and lofty hymns the throne and equipage of God's Almightiness."

The origin of *Paradise Lost* has been ascribed by some to the poet having read Andreini's drama of *L'Adamo, Sacra repre-sentatione*, published at Milan, 1613; by others, to his perusal of Jacobus de Theramo's *Das Buch Belial*, etc., 1472. Yet another theory insists that the *prima stamina* of the great epic is to be found in Sylvester's translation of Du Bartas's *Divine Weekes and Workes.* It is said that Milton himself admitted that he owed much of his work to Phineas Fletcher's *Locustes or Apollyonists.* He is also supposed to have derived inspiration for his great epic from a volume entitled *The Glasse of Time*, by J. Peyton, 1609.

In the year 1654, four years before Milton began *Paradise Lost*, the famous Dutch poet Vondel, who was recognized by the Writers' Guild as the head of native letters, and had a reputation far beyond the limits of the Netherlands, published a drama called *Lucifer*, whose main theme was the rebellion of the angels and their overthrow by the armies of God under the leadership of the archangel Michael. Mr. Edmundson is not by any means the first to indicate Milton's use of this drama, but he puts the proofs for the first time before readers of English, and then seeks to show, "not only that the language and imagery of the *Lucifer* exercised a powerful and abiding influence on the mind of Milton, and have left indelible traces upon the pages of the *Paradise Lost*, but that other writings of Vondel can be shown to have affected in no slight or inconsiderable degree all the great poems of Milton's later life."

Milton did use the ideas of Vondel largely. But he also used the ideas of others, English, Italian, Roman, and Greek, and justified himself in the famous sentence, " Borrowing, if it be not bettered by the borrower, is accounted plagiarie," leaving it to be understood that, if ever he himself borrowed from others, in all cases he improved the matter taken.

A study of the origins of *Paradise Lost* and *Samson Agonistes*, which leads directly over into Holland, is peculiarly interesting to Americans, since these poems appeared when the Atlantic seaboard was freshly peopled by colonies from Holland and Great Britain. It is in every way a matter that touches us nationally and ancestrally. The Pilgrims, like the Huguenots, who, with the Dutch, founded the Eastern States, were all more or less affected by Dutch religious questions, Dutch politics, and Dutch thought. They found refuge in Holland, and were helped by Dutchmen. Milton is the great Puritan poet who belongs to New England quite as much as to Old. But another curious link in the chain is the fact that Roger Williams, of Rhode Island, during his return to London, taught Milton that Dutch language which he immediately put to use, not only in polemics against Salmasius and Morus, but in reading and digesting the religio-satiric plays and epics of Joost van den Vondel.

Milton has been compared to the nightingale because he warbled his stately harmonies in his blindness ; and, on account of his loss, to the bird of Paradise, which, flying against the wind, best displays the splendour of its plumage. Or, as Gray has beautifully apostrophised him, as one

> " who rode sublime
> Upon the seraph wings of ecstasy,—
> The secret of the abyss to spy ;
> Who passed the flaming bounds of space and time,—
> The living throne, the sapphire's blaze,
> Where angels tremble while they gaze !
> He saw,—but, blasted with excess of light,
> Closed his eyes in endless night."

6

Milton did not commence the composition of his grand epic until he was forty-seven years of age, although he had matured his plan for the work several years previously. Milton's epic was formed out of the first draft of a tragedy to which he had given the title of *Adam Unparadised.*

Paradise Regained is attributed to the poet having been asked by Elwood the Quaker what he could say on the subject. " Thou hast given us *Paradise Lost ;* hast thou nothing to say of *Paradise Found ?* " was the demand of Elwood the Quaker, to whom the world is so deeply indebted for his care of the poet, for carrying him to the house of one of his friends in a genial climate, some distance from the plague-stricken city in which he habitually dwelt ; most of all for the answer which he obtained to his appropriate and well-timed question.

Milton used to sit leaning backward obliquely in an easy chair ; he frequently composed in bed in the morning, but when he could not sleep and lay awake whole nights, not one verse could he

make; at other times flowed easy his un-
premeditated lines, with a certain impetus,
as he himself used to believe. Then, whatever the hour, he rang for his daughter
to commit them to paper. He would
sometimes dictate forty lines in a breath,
and then reduce them to half the number.

There is no spectacle in the history of
literature more touching and sublime than
Milton—blind, poor, persecuted and
alone, "fallen upon evil days and evil
tongues, in darkness and with dangers
compassed round"—retiring into obscurity to compose those immortal epics,
Paradise Lost and *Paradise Regained*,
which have placed him among the greatest
poets of all time. The *Paradise Lost* was
originally comprised in ten books; subsequently the work was divided into
twelve. The composition of the work
occupied the poet seven years.

In his twenty-third year the poet was
living with his father at Horton, in Buckinghamshire; there he continued to reside
for five years. In those years he wrote
L'Allegro and *Il Penseroso, Comus, The
Arcades,* and *Lycidas.*

The *Comus* of Milton was suggested by the circumstance of Lady Egerton losing her way in a wood.

Milton was one of the principal pioneers, with his pen, in the sacred cause of liberty, as well as our " poet of Paradise." In his latter character, Wilmott pictures him to us as " walking up and down, in his sing-ing robes, in the cities of many lands ; having his home and his welcome in every devout heart, and upon every learned tongue of the Christian world."

The endowment of genius is from the same Divine source that imparted fragrance and beauty to the flower, and song and plumage to the bird.

> " The heart that suffers most, may sing,—
> All beauty seems of sorrow born ;
> This truth, half seen in life's young morn,
> Stands full and clear at evening :
> The gems of thought most highly prized,
> Are tears of sorrow crystallized."

The author of *Night Thoughts*, unlike most of his brother-bards, seemed to prefer the shady side of life ; yet this gloomy proclivity of his pen is the more singular from the fact that he was far from being insensible to life's genial influences and enjoyments. One day walking in his garden in company with two ladies, one of whom he afterwards married, his servant came to announce a visitor who wished to see him. "Tell him I am too happily engaged to change my situation," was his reply. His fair companions insisted that he should obey the summons, and they took him to the garden gate, when finding further resistance vain, he bowed to them, and improvised these lines :—

"Thus Adam looked, when from the garden driven,
　And thus disputed orders sent from Heaven;
　Like him, I go, but yet to go I'm loath,—
　Like him, I go, for angels drove us both :
　Hard was his fate, but mine still more unkind,—
　His Eve went with him, but mine stays behind ! "

Notwithstanding the morbid spirit which pervades and overshadows much of his poetry, depriving it somewhat of its potency, it yet abounds with grand imagery and impressive eloquence. Had the poet but infused a little star-light into his *Night Thoughts* they would have possessed a tenfold charm.

Edward Young, who was chaplain to George II. in 1728, had the misfortune not only to lose by death his young wife, but also two other members of his family circle; and to this triple bereavement is to be ascribed its sombre hue, as well as the composition of his poem ; which was published in 1746.

The latest and best story of Johnson's *Dictionary* is by Mr. H. B. Wheatley,[1] from which we cite the following :—

"Johnson was one day sitting in Robert Dodsley's shop, when the bookseller took occasion to observe that a dictionary of the English language would be a work that would be well received by the public. Johnson caught at the idea, but after a pause said, 'I believe I shall not undertake it.' A few years after the publication of the great work, he said to Boswell, 'Dodsley first mentioned to me the scheme of an English dictionary, but I had long thought of it.' Dodsley took great interest in the progress of the work he had suggested, and he appears to have supplied Johnson with those collections of Pope which are referred to in the *Plan*, where we read : 'Many of the writers whose testimonies will be alleged were selected by Mr. Pope, of whom I may be justified in affirming that were he still alive, solicitous as he was for the success of this work, he would not be displeased that I have undertaken it.' Dodsley also thought that the work would gain in credit with the public if it were put under the patronage of the Earl of Chesterfield, and he induced Johnson to address the *Plan,* which appeared in 1747, to that noble- man. Whatever work Johnson may have done at that time in collection of materials, there can be no doubt that he had thoroughly thought out his scheme. The *Plan* is a masterly production, which can be read with pleasure, for the elegance of its composition and the justness of its criticism. It opens with a certain mock humility, in which spirit the author shows in the strongest terms the low estimation in which his vocation was held by the public, with the evident intention of raising that vocation by his own performance. This he has done so successfully, that the title of lexico- grapher is given as the highest honour to one of our greatest writers. Between the years 1747 and 1755 Johnson slaved away at his arduous labours, and Lord Chesterfield forgot the very existence of his humble correspondent, to be awakened when it became known that the Dictionary was nearly ready for publication. ' The patron ' wrote two articles in the *World,* where in a light and airy tone he recommended the work to the public, and suggested that Johnson should be accepted as dic- tator of the English language. The reply to these soft blandishments came quick and sharp in the form of a scathing letter written in the most mag- nificent English, which will be read to the end of time with pleasure by all those who are interested in the dignity of literature. Carlyle called this letter 'the far-famed blast of doom, proclaiming into the ears of Lord Chesterfield, and through him of the listening world, that patronage should be no more.'"

In his Preface to the *Dictionary* Johnson thus refers to his mode of selection of terms and words :—

"When I took the first survey of my undertaking, I found our speech copious without order, and energetic without rule. Wherever I turned my view there was perplexity to be disentangled, and confusion to be regulated: choice was to be made out of boundless variety, without any established principles of selection ; adulterations were to be detected, without a settled test of purity; and modes of expression to be rejected or received without the suffrages of any writers of classical reputation or acknowledged authority."

In the scathing retort upon his *quasi* patron, Lord Chesterfield, Johnson writes :

"Seven years, my lord, have now passed since I waited in your outward rooms, or was repulsed from your door; during which time I have been pushing on my work through difficulties of which it is useless to complain, and have brought it at last to the verge of publication, without one act of assistance, one word of encouragement, or one

smile of favour.   Such treatment I did not expect,
for I never had a patron before.   Is not a patron,
my lord, one who looks with unconcern on a man
struggling for life in the water, and when he has
reached ground, encumbers him with help ?"

And then, referring to the number of
persons who, for fifty years, were occupied on the great French dictionary,
while he worked single-handed, he con-
cludes with a pathos unsurpassable :—

" I may sure be contented without praise of
perfection which, if I could obtain in this gloom
of solitude, what would it avail ?   I have protracted my work till most of those whom I wished
to please have sunk into the grave, and success
and miscarriage are empty sounds.   I therefore
dismiss it with frigid tranquillity, having nothing
to fear or hope from censure or from praise."

No sooner, however, did the *Dictionary*
appear, than it was greeted by the public with unbounded favour.

Boswell's account of the manner in
which Johnson compiled his *Dictionary*
is confused.   He seems, according to
another authority, to have begun the
Herculean task by devoting himself to
a diligent study of such English writers
as were most correct in their use of

language, and under every sentence which he meant to quote, he drew a line, and noted in the margin the first letter of the word under which it was to occur. He then delivered these books to his assistants, who transcribed each sentence on a separate slip of paper, and arranged the same under the word referred to. By this method he collected the several words with their different significations; and when the whole arrangement was alphabetically formed, he gave the definitions of their meanings, and collected their etymologies, from Skinner, Junius, and other writers on the subject.

Dodsley, with other booksellers, contracted with Johnson, single and unaided, for the execution of the colossal work in three years, for the sum of fifteen hundred and seventy-five pounds.

Johnson's general habit of composing was to commit to memory what authors usually put on record with pen and paper; this was his custom in consequence of his defect of sight. He wrote *The Vanity of Human Wishes*, being the tenth satire of *Juvenal* imitated, with wonderful rapidity, composing on one occasion seventy lines without putting them to paper until he had completed them.

Then, his uncommonly retentive memory enabled him to deliver a whole essay, properly finished, whenever it was called for. Sir John Hawkins informs us that his essays hardly ever underwent a revision before they went to the press; and adds :—

"The original manuscripts of the *Rambler* have passed through my hands, and by the perusal of them I am warranted to say, as was said of Shakespeare by the players of his time, that he *never blotted a line.*"

Johnson's latest, if not his best, work was his *Lives of the Poets*, originating in the proposal made to him by several publishers that he should write a few lines of biographical and critical preface to the collected works of the English poets, of which they were preparing an edition.

Johnson himself tells us he has written a hundred lines of verse in a day :—

"I remember I wrote a hundred lines of *The Vanity of Human Wishes* in a day."

Referring to his work on his *Dictionary*, his friend Adams asked him how he expected to accomplish it in three years, since the French Academy, consisting of forty members, took forty years to compile their *Dictionary*. Johnson replied :—

"Sir, thus it is : this is the proportion ; forty times forty is sixteen hundred. As three to sixteen hundred, so is the proportion of an Englishman to a Frenchman !"

The laborious work necessary for the production of his great *Dictionary*, which Dr. Johnson undertook to complete in three years, occupied eight, in writing, correcting, and revising. After thirty years of intense devotion to literature, George III. honoured him with a pension of three hundred pounds a year, and thus rescued him from the pressure of pecuniary embarrassments. Johnson's well-known poem, *The Vanity of Human Wishes*,—which was the admiration of Byron and Scott,—alone may assign to him a niche in the poetic Pantheon.

Johnson must have had a certain grim pleasure when he put into words what he supposed to be the popular opinion of the dictionary-maker :—

"Lexicographer: A writer of dictionaries, a harmless drudge that busies himself in tracing the origin and detailing the signification of words."

In the first edition of his *Dictionary* in two hnge folio volumes are to be found queer and obsolete terms, and such odd explanations as that under the word *Network*,—"Anything reticulated or decussated, at equal distances, with interstices between the intersections."

Carlyle has, with his customary vigour and fidelity, given us his estimate of Johnson's great knowledge of mankind, and his skilful analysis of individual character, when he writes :—

"Few men have seen more clearly into the motives, the interests, the whole walk and conversation of the living busy world as it lay before him. And to estimate the quantity of work that Johnson has performed, how much poorer the world were had it wanted him, can, as in all such cases, never be accurately done ; cannot, till after some longer space, be approximately done. All work is a seed sown ; it grows and spreads, and sows itself anew, and so, in endless palingenesia, lives and works. To Johnson's writings, good and solid, and still profitable as they are, we have rated his life and conversation as superior. By the one and by the other, who shall compute what effects have been produced, and are still, and into deep time, producing?"

His sagacious words and suggestions are likely to last with the literature of the language, for they embody great living truths and principles which are and must continue superior to the changes which affect and rule in the minor affairs of life.

Johnson—who did so much to lift up and dignify the literary profession—insisted that "the chief glory of every people arises from its authors." And he yet somewhere puts the strange inquiry,—Was there ever anything written by mere man, that was wished longer by its readers, excepting *Don Quixote, Robinson Crusoe,* and the *Pilgrim's Progress?* If these were his pet books, yet he was an omnivorous devourer of all sorts of books himself.

Among the uses of biographies of distinguished persons is that they occasionally furnish to us glimpses of their domestic habits and characteristic pursuits. We are interested in even the minor incidents of their lives, for these often contribute to make up the psychological sketch. It is when thus admitted to a private view of their home-life that we are enabled to form a just estimate of their character. It is the small talk and gossip of Boswell's *Life of Johnson* that is its charm, and that constitutes it such a universal favourite. Boswell has so industriously collected the foolish as well as the wise observations of the great lexicographer, portrayed his asperities as well as his amenities, his eccentricities as well as excellences, so faithfully, that we are at no loss to estimate his character. Let who will question the accuracy of taste discovered in such minute disclosures, it cannot be denied that they are the very details essential to a true portrait.

Gray, who, it has been said, was "saturated with the finest essence of the Attic muse," wrote his famous *Ode*, founded upon the Welsh tradition that when Edward I. conquered the Principality, he ordered the bards to be put to death.

Of Gray's *Elegy* it is related that General Wolfe, on the evening preceding the memorable battle of the Plains of Abraham, repeated the noble and seemingly prophetic line—

"The paths of glory lead but to the grave!"

to his brother officers, adding: "Now, gentlemen, I would rather be author of that poem than take Quebec!" There are two manuscripts of the *Elegy* in existence ; one containing five stanzas which the author never inserted in the published editions. Gray, with a friend, once saw an elegant book-case filled with a choice collection of French classics, handsomely bound, the price of which was one hundred guineas. He expressed a strong desire for this lot, but could not then afford to buy it. The conversation between the poet and his friend being overheard by the Duchess of Northumberland, who was acquainted with the latter, she took the opportunity of ascertaining who his friend was. Upon finding that it was Gray the poet, she at once bought the bookcase, with its contents, and sent it to his lodgings, with a note, importing that she was—

"ashamed of sending so small an acknowledgment for the infinite pleasure she had received in reading the *Elegy in a Country Churchyard*, of all others her most favourite poem."

That oft-quoted couplet—

"Where ignorance is bliss,
'Tis folly to be wise,"

we derive from his *Ode to Eton College.*

Gray began his *Elegy* soon after the death of his friend Richard West, about 1742 ; it is supposed the event prompted the poem. It was laid aside, however, for nearly seven years, and in 1750 was resumed, when the poet thus referred to the circumstance in his letter to Walpole :—

"I have been here at Stoke a few days (where I shall continue good part of the summer), and having put an end to a thing whose beginning you have seen long ago, I immediately send it you. You will, I hope, look upon it in the light of a thing with an end to it,—a merit that most of my writings have wanted, and are like to want."

The *Elegy* was much handed about in manuscript, and, like Coleridge's *Christabel*, in that condition gained considerable celebrity. In 1751 it was ascertained that it was likely to be published without his consent, and Gray desired Walpole to place his copy in Dodsley's hands, to be printed and published, with this direction :—

"Print it without any interval between the stanzas, because the sense is, in some places, continued beyond them; and the title must be *Elegy Written in a Country Churchyard.* If he would add a line or two, to say it came into his hands by accident, I should like it better."

It has not been ascertained how long Gray was engaged upon the structure of the *Elegy*, although he is known to have made frequent revisions and alterations of it. The actual locality of its composition is, we believe, as yet undetermined; there is a tradition that it was within the precincts of the church of Granchester, about two miles from Cambridge; and the "curfew" is supposed to have been the great bell of St. Mary's.

It would be superfluous to speak of the

merits of this matchless poem, its world-
wide popularity evinces how universally it
charms and impresses the reader. It has
been translated into Hebrew, Greek, Latin,
French, Italian, Portuguese, German, and
reprinted more frequently in the original
than almost any other prodúction of its
class.

Campbell's *Pleasures of Hope*, written
in 1799, when its author was only twenty-
two years of age, is mainly indebted to its
beautiful episodes for its protracted popularity. His *Hohenlinden*, by some considered his finest lyric, was yet rejected by
a sapient editor of Greenock, and even the
poet himself would not admit its merit.

Campbell in a letter thus refers to the
impressions he received of the battle of
Hohenlinden, upon which his splendid lyric
was founded :—

"Never shall time efface from my memory the
recollection of that hour of astonishment and
suspended breath, when I stood with the good
monks of St. Jacob, to overlook a charge of
Klenau's cavalry upon the French under Grenier,
encamped below us. We saw the fire given and
returned, and heard distinctly the sound of the
French *pas de charge*, collecting the lines to attack

in close column. After three hours awaiting the issue of a severe action, a park of artillery was opened just beneath the walls of the monastery, and several waggoners, who were stationed to convey the wounded in spring waggons, were killed in our sight. My love of novelty now gave way to personal fear ; and I took a carriage, in company with an Austrian surgeon, back to Landshut. I remember," he adds, on his return to England, "how little I valued the art of painting before I got into the heart of such impressive scenes ; but in Germany I would have given anything to have possessed an art capable of conveying ideas inaccessible to speech and writing. Some particular scenes were rather overcharged with that degree of the terrific which oversteps the sublime ; and I own my flesh yet creeps at the recollection of spring waggons and hospitals ; but the sight of Ingoldstadt in ruins, or Hohenlinden covered with fire seven miles in circumference, were spectacles never to be forgotten."

It is related of Campbell that shortly before his death he read before the assemblage at the opening of the Exhibition in Suffolk Place, London, that grand piece the *Thanatopsis* of Bryant, and broke down with emotion when he came to the lines—

" So live, that when thy summons comes to join
The innumerable caravan that moves

To the pale realms of shade, where each shall
  take
His chamber in the silent halls of Death,
Thou go not like the quarry-slave, at night
Scourged to his dungeon," etc. ;—

saying that nothing finer had ever been written.

The oft-cited line of Campbell—

"Like angel-visits, few and far between,"

has been traced back to Norris of Bemerton ; it occurs in the following beautiful stanza :—

" How fading are the joys we dote upon ;
  Like apparitions seen and gone ;
  But those who soonest take their flight,
  Are the most exquisite and strong,—
  Like angel-visits short and bright,—
  Mortality's too weak to bear them long."

The comparison of human joys to the visits of angels, after having been engrafted into the *Grave* of Blair, was transferred by Campbell to his *Pleasures of Hope,* and has long since passed into a poetic proverb.

V.

Goldsmith. — Cowper. — Burns. —
Sterne.— Richardson. —Fielding.—
Smollett.—Beckford's " Vathek."—
Wordsworth. — Scott. —Coleridge.
—Audubon.—Wilson.

NTIL comparatively recent times
it was supposed that Goldsmith's
Vicar of Wakefield was suggested
by an anonymous work entitled *The Journal
of a Wiltshire Curate,* but the former having been published in March 1766, and
the latter not appearing in print until the
following December; and further, Goldsmith having written other papers in the
British Magazine, in which both works
appeared, the supposition of plagiarism, of
course, ceases to be possible.

The ballad of *Edwin and Angelina* was
originally written and privately printed for
the amusement of the Countess of North-

umberland, and was afterwards inserted in the *Vicar of Wakefield.*

The Vicar of Wakefield was much admired by Moore, who read it to his wife; and Scott tells us he returned to it again and again, and blessed the memory of its author. Carlyle designates it "the best of modern idyls;" and Goethe declared in his eighty-first year that the *Vicar of Wakefield* was his delight at the age of twenty, and that he had recently read it again, with a renewed delight, and with a grateful sense of the early benefit he had derived from it.

While engaged with Newberry the publisher, Goldsmith lodged with a Mrs. Fleming, and it was in her lodgings that being pressed either to pay his bill or to marry his landlady, Goldsmith applied to Dr. Johnson. On that occasion the manuscript of the *Vicar of Wakefield* was produced; and Johnson was so much pleased with it that he obtained sixty pounds for the work, and thus rescued its poor author from the embarrassed situation in which he was placed by Mrs. Fleming. This incident is all the more interesting since from such a seeming accident should have sprung one of the most cherished of the literary gems of our language.

Goldsmith composed his *Deserted Village* whilst staying at a farmhouse nearly opposite the church at Springfield, Essex. The village, which he calls Auburn, was *Lissoy*, where in his youth every spot was familiar to him, as well as the places and also characters then living there, and whom he has sketched in the poem. The schoolmaster was a sketch from life, one Paddy Burn, a man "severe to view;" and so was the keeper of the alehouse where

> " Imagination fondly stoops to trace
> The parlour splendours of that festive place."

Every one knows Boswell's carefully-worded account of the romantic circumstances in which Johnson relieved Goldsmith's distress by selling the manuscript of his novel to some unnamed bookseller for £60. Boswell's story is professedly Johnson's "own exact version," and corrects what he calls the "strangely misstated" facts of Mrs. Thrale and Sir John

Hawkins. With these varying accounts Mr. Austin Dobson collates that of Richard Cumberland, and observes, in conclusion : "Boswell's story alone wears an air of veracity, and it has generally been regarded as the accepted version." The novel was published March 27th, 1766, and was advertised in the *Public Advertiser* of the same date, together with *The Traveller*, which was published in 1764.

Mr. Dobson has discovered that as far back as October 28th, 1762, Collins, the Salisbury printer, had purchased of " Dr. Goldsmith, the Author," for £21 a third share in *The Vicar of Wakefield*. This interesting fact is disclosed by an old account book, once belonging to Collins, and now in possession of Mr. Charles Welsh, a member of the firm of publishers successors to John Newberry. Several curious items connected with the sale of the novel are communicated by Mr. Welsh. It appears from the memoranda of Collins that the fourth edition started with a loss, and Collins sold his third share for five guineas.

" The impression has been general that this

immortal work enjoyed a brisk sale, at least in the early editions, and that the original purchaser delayed its publication for some fifteen months. The strange truth is now revealed that for more than three years did its three owners agree to keep it from the light, and that one of them was so hopeless of its permanent value that he sold his share for a paltry sum four years after its publication." [1]

An amusing adventure which occurred in Goldsmith's last journey from his home to Edgeworthstown school is believed to have given birth to the chief incidents in the drama of *She Stoops to Conquer.* Having set off on horseback (a friend having given him a guinea), he, schoolboy-like, thought he would play the gentleman, and meeting a person on his road, inquired for the best inn. His informant, being disposed to a practical joke, directed him to the house of the wealthiest personage of the place. Not suspecting any deception, Oliver proceeded as directed, and on reaching the mansion gave directions about his horse. He was ushered into the presence of the squire, who at once detected the mistake. Being himself fond of a joke, he encouraged the lad in his

[1] *Saturday Review.*

mistake, and at length found by the relation of his history that Goldsmith's father was not unknown to him. Nothing occurred to undeceive the self-important youth until he had dined with the family circle, and on the following morning when he was about to take his departure, on offering to pay for his entertainment he discovered his mistake.

Sir Joshua Reynolds relates an anecdote of Goldsmith, while engaged upon his poem, which may be worth repeating. Calling upon the poet, he opened the door without ceremony, and found him in the double occupation of turning a couplet and teaching a pet dog to stand upon his haunches. At one moment he would glance his eye at the desk and at another shake his finger at the dog to make him retain his position. The last lines on the page were still wet (they form a part of the description of Italy), and are these :—

" By sports like these are all their cares beguiled ;
The sports of children satisfy the child."

A literary friend once recommended Goldsmith to employ an amanuensis, and thereby escape the labour of writing his

MS., and he tried the experiment. He made an arrangement for the scribe's attendance, but, after pacing up and down the room, and "racking his brains" to no purpose, he put the fee into the hand of his amanuensis, saying, "It won't do, my friend; I find that my head and my hand must work together."

The origin of Cowper's comic ballad of *John Gilpin* is well known, but may be repeated here. It happened one afternoon in those years when Cowper's accomplished friend, Lady Austen, made a part of his little social circle, that she observed him looking very dejected, when she told him the story of John Gilpin, which she remembered from childhood. Its effect on the poet was like an enchantment. He informed Lady Austen on the following morning that the recollection of her story had so captivated him that he had during the night turned it into a ballad. Of this ballad, which had, soon after its publication, become the popular talk of the day, and had been read to crowded houses in theatres, Cowper thus speaks in after days :—"The grinners at John

Gilpin little dream what the author sometimes suffers. How I hated myself yesterday for ever having wrote it." To his
friend Lady Austen Cowper was indebted
for the suggestion of the greatest of his
productions, *The Task.*

Who has not read Cowper's touching
lines on "The Receipt of his Mother's
Picture"? The occasion was the receipt
of his mother's portrait from his cousin,
and in a letter to that lady he uses the
following words :—

"The world could not have furnished you with
a present so acceptable to me as the picture which
you have so kindly sent me. I received it the
night before last, and viewed it with a trepidation
of nerves and spirits somewhat akin to what I
should have felt had the dear original presented
herself to my embraces. I kissed it and hung it
where it is the last object that I see at night, and,
of course, the first on which I open my eyes in the
morning."

"It is incorrect to say that Cowper's malady
was religious mania ; on the contrary, to his strong
religious sentiment was due the consolation of
many an hour, lightening its darkness and cheer-
ing its sorrow, standing as a guardian angel
between him and the cell of the raging lunatic and

the suicide's grave. And so let us leave him, with his own words still fresh in our memory : 'Such was the goodness of the Lord, that He gave me the oil of joy for mourning, and the garments of praise for the spirit of heaviness.' The claim of Cowper to be considered a poet of great excellence has been 'long and indisputably established ; and he may be considered, like Goldsmith, as a precursor of that style of poetry which appeals to the great interests of humanity in a rational, philosophical spirit. His pictures of social life are as truthful as they are charming."[1]

To the poet of the domestic virtues, Cowper, are we indebted for having brought the Muse, in her most attractive guise, to sit down by our hearths, and breathe a sanctity over the daily economy of human life. His poetry influences the feelings as a summer day affects the body, imparting to the mind a sense of calm enjoyment and happiness.

" I would forgive a man for not reading Milton," once said Charles Lamb, " but I would not call that man my friend who should be offended with the divine chit-chat of Cowper."

He wrote pieces which have given consolation to all classes of Christians, yet

[1] Waller's *Boswell.*

he himself took no comfort from them. His last piece, *The Castaway*, which shows no decay of mental power, though he was then in his seventieth year, is among the most touching poems in any language. He had been reading in Anson's *Voyages* an account of a man lost overboard in a gale.

A curious illustration of erratic criticism may be seen in the case of *Cowper's Poems*. A portion of his poems was offered in manuscript to Johnson, the publisher, on conditions that he should assume the risk of publication.

"The publisher read the MSS., approved of them, and published them in a volume. But the erudite critics condemned the work as utterly devoid of merit, and nearly the whole edition remained unsold. After a year or more a relative of the poet called again upon the publisher with another batch of manuscripts, which he offered on the same terms. and they were accepted as before. This was the MS. of *The Task;* and no sooner did this volume make its appearance than the reviewers hailed Cowper as the first poet of the age, and this success set the first work in motion. Johnson, his publisher, was courageous and of good critical judgment, wiser than his first censors, and he reaped his reward, for it is estimated that in two years the copyright of Cowper's poems produced the then large sum of six thousand seven hundred and sixty-four pounds ! " [1]

Cowper is less read than he deserves to be, but he has this glory, that he has ever been the favourite poet of deeply religious minds ; and his history is peculiarly touching, as that of one who, himself plunged in despair and madness, has brought hope and consolation to a thousand other souls.

" O poets, from a maniac's tongue was poured the
    deathless singing ;
  O Christians, to your cross of hope a hopeless
    hand was clinging ;
  O men, this man in brotherhood your weary
    hearts beguiling,
  Groaned inly while he gave you peace, and died
    while ye were smiling.

  He shall be strong to sanctify the poet's high
    vocation ;
  And bow the meekest Christian down in meeker
    adoration ;
  Nor ever shall he be in love by wise and good
    forsaken—
  Named softly as the household name of one
    whom God hath taken ! " [2]

While the sweet melodies of Cowper

[1] Timbs.   [2] Canon Farrar.

were filling hearts and homes with their music, a rustic peasant of Scotia was tuning his reed to "A Mountain Daisy," or chanting his love-plaints to some fairy-footed nymph beside some Scottish stream. It is not an easy thing to find out the sources of his inspiration; for the most part they were, doubtless, his love of nature and of his fair friends. Burns was little more than sixteen years old when he wrote some of his most remarkable lyrics; and the brief limit of thirty-seven years made up the short span of the poet's life,—a life so prolific of pleasure to the world, yet so checkered and unpropitious to himself.

One of Burns's most pathetic of lyrics is that entitled " To Mary in Heaven " :—

" Thou ling'ring star, with less'ning ray,
  That lov'st to greet the early morn,
Again thou usher'st in the day
  My Mary from my soul was torn.
O Mary ! dear departed shade !
  Where is thy place of blissful rest ?
See'st thou thy lover lowly laid ?
  Hear'st thou the groans that rend his breast?"

The poet and his rustic maiden met for the last time in a sequestered spot on the

8

banks of the Ayr. Standing on either side of a purling brook, and holding a Bible between them, they exchanged their plighted vows. Mary presented her Bible to the poet, and he gave her his. This Bible has been preserved, and on a blank leaf, in Burns's handwriting, is inscribed, " And ye shall not swear by My name falsely ; I am the Lord," and on another blank leaf his name is written. The lovers never met again, Mary having died suddenly at Greenock ; and over her grave a monument has been erected. On the third anniversary of her death, Jean Armour, then his wife, noticed that towards evening

"he grew sad about something, went into the barnyard, where he strode restlessly up and down for some time, although repeatedly asked to come in. Immediately on entering the house, he sat down and wrote this touching poem, which Lockhart characterises as 'the noblest of all his ballads.' "

Gilbert Burns gives the following account of the origin of " The Cotter's Saturday Night " :—

" Robert had frequently remarked to me," he

says, "that he thought there was something peculiarly venerable in the phrase, 'Let us worship God,' used by a head of a family, introducing family worship. To this sentiment of the author the world is indebted for this poem. We used frequently to walk together on Sunday afternoons ; and it was on one of these occasions that I first had the pleasure of hearing the author repeat ' The Cotter's Saturday Night.' The 'Cotter' is an exact copy of my father in his manners, and yet the other parts of the description do not apply to our family."

Burns wrote his famous " Tam O'Shanter" almost impromptu, for he is said to have composed it in a single day. The poet was lingering by the river-side a long time, and his wife and children went out to join him ; but perceiving that her presence was an interruption to him, she retired from him. Her attention was, however, attracted by his wild gesticulations and ungovernable mirth while he was reciting the passages of the poem as they arose in his mind. The piece was suggested by a Scottish legend, which the poet gives in one of his letters to his friend Captain Grose ; and the name was derived from an incident in the life of Douglas Grahame of Shanter, a farmer on the Carrick shore, who was, it seems, addicted to libations deep.

"Should auld acquaintance be forgot," or, as its title reads, " Auld Lang Syne," was described by Burns as being—

"an old song and tune which had often thrilled through his soul ; and he professed to his friend Thomson to have received it from an old man's singing, and exclaimed regarding it, ' Light be the turf on the breast of the Heaven-inspired poet who composed this glorious fragment.'"

The second and third verses, however are known to be his own.

Among the books which took the strongest hold on the imagination of Burns were two which filled him with a desire to become a soldier ; these were a Life of Hannibal and a Life of Wallace ; and doubtless to the study of the latter may be attributed his noble lyric, " Scots wha hae wi' Wallace bled."

With regard to the origin of this stirring lyric, which he entitles " Bannockburn," we have the poet's own words as follows :—

"There is a tradition, which I have met with in many places of Scotland, that it was Robert

Bruce's march, at the battle of Bannockburn ; and I do not know whether it was the old air, ' Hey tullie, tailie,' but well I know that with Frazer's hautboy, it has often filled my eyes with tears. This thought, in my solitary wanderings, warmed to a pitch of enthusiasm on the theme of liberty and independence, which I threw into a kind of Scottish ode, fitted to the air that one might suppose to be the gallant Royal Scot's address to his heroic followers, on that eventful morning."

The verses " To a Mouse," and those "To a Mountain Daisy," were composed while their author was holding the plough. Holding the plough was Burns's best time, it is stated, for poetic inspiration—as, indeed, some of his best poems prove. The field on the farm of Mossgiel is still pointed out and visited as the scene of many of the productions of the great Scottish peasant-poet.

Burns tells us that he never feared an enemy or failed a friend, and that " for the rest," he adds :—

" I have written my heart in my poems ; and rude and unfinished and hasty as they are, it can be read there. From seven years of age to this very hour, I have been dependent only on my own head and hands for everything—for very bread. But I thank God that though I felt sad suffering, the scathing blast neither blunted my perceptions of natural and moral beauty, nor, by withering the affections of my heart, made me a selfish man."

His beautiful, brief lyric, " Ae fond kiss," was the tribute of the poet's brain and heart to his Clarinda; everyone admires the little poetic gem, it is so natural an outburst of affection. The poets have acknowledged its beauty; Byron and Scott, as well as Mrs. Anna Jameson, are among its admirers.

"It is a remarkable fact, that the mass of the poetry which has given this extraordinary man his principal fame, burst from him in a comparatively small space of time, not exceeding fifteen months. It began to flow of a sudden, and it ran into one impetuous, brilliant stream, till it seemed to have become comparatively exhausted." [1]

Carlyle regarded Burns's songs as—

" by far the best that Britain has yet produced. Independent of the clear, manly, heart-felt sentiment that ever pervades *his* poetry, his songs are honest in another point of view; in form as well as in spirit. They do not *affect* to be set to music, but they actually and in themselves are music; they have received their life, and fashioned themselves together, in the medium of Harmony, as

[1] Chambers.

Venus rose from the bosom of the sea. If we further take into account the immense variety of his subjects; how from the loud-flowing revel in 'Willie brew'd a peck o' Malt,' to the still, rapt enthusiasm of sadness for 'Mary in Heaven;' from the glad kind greeting of 'Auld Lang Syne,' or the comic archness of 'Duncan Gray,' to the fire-eyed fury of 'Scots wha hae wi' Wallace bled,' he has found a tone and words for every mood of man's heart,—it will seem a small praise if we rank him as the first of all our song-writers, for we know not where to find one worthy of being second to him."

" Such graves as his are pilgrim-shrines, shrines
    to no code or creed confined,—
The Delphian vales, the Palestines, the Meccas,
    of the mind !
They linger by the Doon's low trees, the pastoral
    Nith, the wooded Ayr,
And round thy sepulchres, Dumfries ! the poet's
    tomb is there.
But what to the sculptor's art, his funeral columns,
    wreaths, and urns ?
Wear they not graven on the heart the name of
    Robert Burns?" [1]

Gibbon himself informs us of the circumstances which led to his writing the *Decline and Fall of the Roman Empire,* thus :—

[1] Fitz-Greene Halleck.

" It was at Rome, as I sat musing amidst the ruins of the Capitol, October 15th, 1764,—while the barefooted friars were singing vespers in the temple of Jupiter, that the idea of writing the decline and fall of the city first started to my mind. It was on the day, or rather night, of the 27th June, 1787, between the hours of eleven and twelve o'clock, that I wrote the last lines of the last page, in a summer-house in my garden."

He continues :—

" I will add two facts which have seldom occurred in composition of six, or at least five quartos,—my first rough manuscript, without any intermediate copy, has been sent to the press ; second, not a sheet has been seen by any human eye, except those of the author and the printer,—the faults and merits are exclusively my own."

Gibbon tells us of his History :—

" At the outset, all was dark and doubtful,—even the title of the work, the true era of the decline and fall of the Empire, the limits of the introduction, the division of the chapters and the order of the narration : and I was often tempted to cast away the labour of seven years."

The memoirs of his life reveal to us a picture of his untiring industry, and persistent devotion to his great work, covering a space of nearly a score of years.

His famous work was declined by several publishers, and when undertaken by Cadell, only five hundred copies were at first printed; larger impressions, however, soon followed, in rapid succession, until, as Gibbon says, his book "was on every table and almost every toilette."

Tristram Shandy was condemned by Horace Walpole as "a very insipid and tedious performance;" yet this was Sterne's greatest work. Dodsley, the publisher, gave him six hundred and fifty pounds for the second edition of the work, and two more volumes; and Warburton gave him a purse of gold, and styled him "the English Rabelais." Although the work appeared anonymously, yet it was known to be Sterne's from the first.

Of Sterne's *Sentimental Journey* there is no history, excepting that the author wrote it from notes made during two journeys in France and Italy.

Richardson's once popular novels were suggested to him by a brother bookseller, as an attractive vehicle for conveying ethical teaching to the subordinate classes of society, as well as exhibiting the ideal characters of fiction. Samuel Richardson—who has been called the founder of the modern novel—published in 1741 his *Pamela*, the story of a rustic beauty's adventures and vicissitudes. It originally sprang from a collection of familiar letters, which he designed as a manual for the improvement of the operative classes. The popularity of this work was remarkable, although this, like all Richardson's works, is extremely voluminous. His greatest novel is *Clarissa Harlowe*, which still is regarded as belonging to the front rank of prose fiction.

By this work Richardson, whom nobody suspected of literary ability, introduced a new class or order in the literature of fiction. He is said to have written the story in his cottage at Hammersmith, during the daytime, and in the evenings he read portions of his manuscript to a few ladies, whom he constituted his censors on his delineations of woman's ways,—which to some of us seem past finding out.

The second prominent novelist of this

period is Fielding, who was described by Byron as "the prose Homer of human nature." In 1742 he produced his first work, *Joseph Andrews*, which was, it is said, designed as a humorous satire upon *Pamela*. His principal book was *Tom Jones*, which has been considered one of the finest examples of its class extant in fiction. Smollett's *Humphrey Clinker* is another novel in the epistolary form, and "the most cordial, comic, and laughable of them all."

In the year 1809 was interred, in the churchyard of St. Martin's-in-the-Fields, the body of one Hew Hewson, who died at the age of eighty-five. He was the original of Hugh Strap, in Smollett's *Roderick Random*. Upwards of forty years he kept a hair-dresser's shop in St. Martin's parish; the walls were hung round with Latin quotations, and he would frequently point out to his customers and acquaintances the several scenes in *Roderick Random* pertaining to himself, which had their origin, not in Smollett's inventive fancy, but in truth and reality. The meeting in a barber's shop at Newcastle-upon-Tyne, the subsequent mistake at the inn, their arrival together in London, and the assistance they experienced from Strap's friend, are all facts. The barber left behind an annotated copy of *Roderick Random*, showing how far we are indebted to the genius of the author, and to what extent the incidents are founded in reality.

Another famous work is Beckford's *Vathek: An Arabian Tale.* This work, which is considered the finest of Oriental romances in prose, as Moore's *Lalla Rookh* is the first of these in verse, was written before its author had completed his twentieth year, and published in 1784. For accuracy of detail, beauty of description, and richly luxuriant imagination, it surpassed even Johnson's *Rasselas*, according to the estimate of Byron and some other critics. This work, although its author was an Englishman, was composed in French,—of which its style is a model, —and afterwards was translated. No clue to the origin of the production seems to exist. It may be noted that Hopes, celebrated novel, *Anastasius ; or, Memoirs of a Modern Greek*, which Beckford, it is known, greatly admired, was not published until 1819. He is said to have written this remarkable story at a *single sitting*. Much of the description of Vathek's palace, and even the Hall of Eblis, was afterwards visibly embodied in the real Fonthill Abbey, of which wonders almost as fabulous were at one time reported and believed. Fonthill Abbey, which had been destroyed by fire, cost the sum of £273,000. The building was in the Gothic style, and was surmounted by a central tower of two hundred and eighty feet in height. The abbey was enriched with the treasures of art and vertu, as well as a choice collection of books.

Wordsworth, whose whole life was devoted to his art, and whose poetry was written amidst the inspiration of mountains and meadows, woodland lakes and rural retreats, must have had few cares, living as he did at Grasmere and afterwards at Rydal Mount, sequestered from the busy haunts of men.

Wordsworth, the pastoral and philosophic bard of Rydal Mount, Westmoreland, reveals to us his love of nature in the following lines :—

" One impulse from a vernal wood may teach you
　　more of man,
　Of moral evil and of good, than all the sages
　　can."

Many of his pastorals " are fresh," as Coleridge once said, " with the morning dew."　When once asked by a visitor where his library was, he replied, " The woods and streams are my books."　So fond was he of wandering over "hill and dale, fountain or fresh shade," that De Quincey has estimated his perambulations as exceeding in dimension the circuit of the globe itself.　He informs us that his fine poem on " Tintern Abbey " was composed after crossing the river Wye, and during a four or five days' ramble about that most picturesque river, in company with his sister.　Not a line of it, however, was either uttered or written down until he reached Bristol. His " Ode on Immortality " has this fine burst of poetic lament on illusions of life and the flight of time :—

"There was a time when meadow, grove, and
     stream,
  The earth, and every common sight, to me
     did seem
Apparelled in celestial light—the glory and the
     freshness of a dream!
  It is not now, as it hath been of yore,—
  Turn wheresoe'er I may, by night or day,
The things which I have seen, I now can see no
     more."

The well-known tale of "Peter Bell" was founded upon an incident which met the eye of the poet in a newspaper, of an ass being found hanging its head over a canal in a wretched condition. Upon examination it was ascertained that it was looking and waiting for its master, who had fallen into the water and was drowned. Another of Wordsworth's poems, "The Brothers," was suggested by the following incident, which had been told him up Ennerdale. A shepherd had fallen asleep upon the top of a rock, called the Pillar, and there perished, as described in the poem, his staff having been left mid-way on the cliff. It was of this poem that Southey, in writing to Coleridge, said, "God bless Wordsworth for that poem!" Coleridge confessed to another friend that he "never read that model of English pastoral with an unclouded eye."

It is the high prerogative of the poet to extract, by the alembic of his genius, beautiful thoughts and images from the minute and even commonplace things, as well as the grander and more sublime aspects of nature. Few objects in the arcana of nature more readily attract the eye of the poet than the bloom and beauty of the perfumed flowers.

As an illustration of the fact of un-conscious possession of the poetic gift, it is related of Sir Walter Scott that not long before his *Lay of the Last Minstrel* made its appearance, he was crossing the Firth of Forth in a ferry-boat with a friend, and the two proposed to beguile the time by writing a number of verses on given subjects. At the end of an hour's cogitations, they presented the results, when Scott and his friend only produced between them six lines! "It is plain," the former exclaimed, "that you and I need never think of getting our living by writing poetry." Yet who made more money and fame by his genius than did Sir Walter Scott?

An interesting story is furnished by Lockhart of the gradual growth of *The Lay of the Last Minstrel.* The lovely Countess of Dalkeith hears a wild legend of Border *diablerie,* and sportively asks Scott to make it the subject of a ballad. The poet's accidental confinement in the midst of a yeomanry camp gave him leisure to meditate his theme to the sound of the bugle; suddenly there flashes on him the idea of extending his simple outline so as to embrace a vivid panorama of that old Border life of war and tumult. A friend's suggestion led to the arrangement and framework of the *Lay* and the conception of the ancient Harper. Thus step by step grew the poem that first made its author famous.

Of the three poems, *The Lady of the Lake, Marmion,* and the *Lay of the Last Minstrel,* the last named is considered to bear the palm of excellence. The *Lay,* however, was modelled after the irregular structure of Coleridge's unfinished poem of *Christabel,* as Scott admits that it was in it he first found this measure used in serious poetry.

Carlyle considers that Scott's first literary effort, the translation of *Götz von Ber-lichengen,* was the prime cause of his *Marmion, Lady of the Lake,* and all that followed from the same creative hand.

The manuscript of *Waverley* lay hid away in an old cabinet for years before the public were aware of its existence. In the words of the Great Unknown : " I had written the greater part of the first volume and sketched other passages, when I mislaid the manuscript ; and only found it by the merest accident, as I was rummaging the drawer of an old cabinet ; and I took the fancy of finishing it."

In the year 1816 the *Antiquary* appeared, and for eight years a long succession of novels emanated from his prolific brain with a rapidity as wonderful as their merits were great. Of the origin of these historic romances the author himself thus informs us :—

" My early recollections of Highland scenery and customs made so favourable an impression in the poem called *The Lady of the Lake,* that I was induced to think of attempting something of the same kind in prose. I had been a good deal in the Highlands at a time when they were much less accessible, and much less visited, than they have been of late years, and was acquainted with many of the old warriors of 1745, who were, like most veterans, easily induced to fight their battles over again, for the benefit of a willing listener like myself. It naturally occurred to me that the ancient traditions and high spirit of a people who, living in a civilised age and country, retained so strong a tincture of manners belonging to an early period of society, must afford a subject favourable for romance, if it should not prove a curious tale marred in the telling. It was with some idea of this kind that, about the year 1805, I threw together about one-third part of the first volume of *Waverley.*"

In Scott's *Ivanhoe* is the character of Rebecca, the original of which was a lady of Philadelphia, named Rebecca Gratz, who was possessed of singular beauty. One of the most intimate friends of her family was Washington Irving, and it is through his acquaintance with this lady and Sir Walter Scott that we have handed down to us the beautiful portraiture that so graces the charming work of that Wizard of the North, *Ivanhoe.* The original of

Jeanie Deans, in the *Heart of Midlothian*, was Helen Walker, a Scottish girl, left an orphan with the charge of a younger sister. The reader is doubtless familiar with the thrilling story of her heroic bravery in saving at the last moment her sister's life, who was condemned to suffer the penalty for murder. Scott wrote the epitaph on the tomb of Helen, whose body lies in the churchyard of Irongray, six miles from Dumfries.

Scott, " the potent wizard of romance, at the waving of whose wand came trooping on the stage of life again gallant knights and ladies fair, exprisoned chargers and splendid tournaments, with their flashing armour and blazoned shields,' was the poet, also, who loved to sing of knightly deeds of valour and old traditional love-lays. He was endowed with such wonderful fertility of invention and facility of composition, that he was compared to a high-pressure engine, the steam of which always was up as soon as he entered his study, which was generally at six a.m. Melrose he has consecrated by his genius, Abbotsford by his living presence,. and

Dryburgh by his sacred dust ; while
Nature herself may be said, in his own
beautiful lines, to do homage to his
memory.

" Call it not vain,—they do not err, who say that
    when the poet dies,
  That Nature mourns her worshipper, and cele-
    brates his obsequies,
    And rivers teach the rushing wave
    To murmur dirges round his grave ! "

Sir Walter himself tells us that the fame
of Miss Edgeworth did much to inspire
him.   He says that her writings did more
than all the legislative enactments towards
completing the union between the Irish
and English peoples.   Scott felt that he
might do for Scotland what Miss Edgeworth had achieved for Ireland—that he
might familiarize Englishmen with the
virtues and foibles of the gallant Scotch
race, and promote a free and unrestrained
intercourse between the two nations.   The
idea ultimately developed itself in the
long and illustrious series known as the
Waverley Novels.

Washington Irving wrote parts of *The
Sketch Book* in London and elsewhere;

his story of *The Stout Gentleman* was sketched while mounted on a stile at Stratford-on-Avon. Irving's love of letters was an intuition ; on one occasion he said, in reference to his fitful muse, "But these capricious moods, of the heat and glow of composition, have been the happiest hours of my life. I have never found, in anything outside of the four walls of my study, any enjoyment equal to sitting at my writing desk, with a clean page, a new theme, and a mind awake." When in Paris he seems to have been unable to do much with his pen for some six weeks, when his friend Moore called upon him. Irving told him how long he had been waiting for the impulse to write something, but that now it had come to him, and he showed him his desk covered with closely written sheets ; that work was *Bracebridge Hall.*

A love of the muse was enkindled in the mind and heart of James Montgomery in his school-days by hearing Blair's "Grave" read. Many of his poems were composed during his unjust imprisonment ; for he was a philanthropist as well as a poet, and because of his conscientious opposition to slavery and other political abuses he became the victim of persecution. He wrote his well-known poem "The Common Lot" during a country walk in the snow. His productions are voluminous, and some of his poems and hymns are great favourites, such as his "Oh, where shall rest be found?" "Night is the time for rest," "There is a calm for those who weep," and "Friend after friend departs! who has not lost a friend?" "Prayer is the soul's sincere desire," etc.

As in the case of Montgomery and others, Leigh Hunt, by the power of his genius, seems to have transfigured the gloomy prison-house into a fairy palace of the imagination ; he wrote in part his *Story of Rimini* and *The Descent of Liberty* while deprived of his personal freedom. Leigh Hunt has, indeed, been styled "the most blithesome prison-bird that ever warbled in a cage."

Coleridge's "Ancient Mariner" has been the subject of extensive criticism, yet—

"Like all his writings, the versification is exquisite: his language puts on every form, it expresses every sound ; he almost writes to the eye and to the ear. This production is a wild, mystical, phantasmagoric narrative, most picturesquely related in the old English ballad measure, and in language to which an air of antiquity is skilfully given in admirable harmony with the spectral character of the events. The whole poem is a splendid dream, filling the ear with the strange and floating melodies of sleep, and the eye with a shifting, vaporous succession of fantastic images, gloomy or radiant." [1]

This weird poem describes a man who shot an albatross, a bird of good omen to sailors. For this offence he was severely punished, and on his repentance was doomed to wander over the earth, and repeat the story of his wrong as a warning to others.

"The poem originated," says Wordsworth, 'out of the want of five pounds which Coleridge and I needed to make a tour together in Devonshire. We agreed to write, jointly, a poem, the subject of which Coleridge took from a dream which a friend of his had once dreamt concerning a person suffering under a dire curse from the commission of some crime. I supplied the crime, the shooting of the albatross, from an accident I had met with in one of Shelvocke's voyages. We tried the poem conjointly for a day or two, but we

[1] Shaw's *English Literature.*

pulled different ways, and only a few lines of it
are mine."

Coleridge's changeful career exhibits
many phases of character, but among them
not the least interesting is that of the poet.
One of the Lake-poets, as they have been
familiarly styled (Wordsworth and Southey
forming with himself the trio), he subsequently removed to Highgate, one of the
northern suburbs of London, ostensibly
for medical treatment of his opium habit.
Instead of being cured, however, it was
hinted that he made his medical friend
as bad as himself. This sad habit in
which he indulged accounts for the strange
mystery of some of his poetry,—" Kubla
Khan," the " Ancient Mariner," and
" Christabel." The " Kubla Khan," which
is so remarkable for its rich delicacy of
colouring, as well as its melody and
mystery, owes its existence to the following
incident. In the summer of 1797 he was
reading in a lonely farm-house, when,
being unwell, he took an anodyne,
from the effects of which he fell asleep
in his chair, at the moment he was reading the following sentence in Purchas's

Pilgrims : " Here the Khan Kubla commanded a palace to be built, and a stately garden thereunto ; and thus ten miles of fertile ground were enclosed with a wall." He continued asleep for three hours, during which time he vividly remembered having composed from two to three hundred lines, and this without any consciousness of effort. On awakening, he remembered the whole, and taking his pen, began eagerly to commit to paper. He had written as far as the published fragment, when he was interrupted by some person on urgent business, which detained him about an hour. On resuming his pen, he was mortified to find that with the exception of a few lines all had vanished from his memory. Coleridge had a wonderful power of summoning up images in his own mind, an instance in point being the lines purporting to have been composed in the valley of Chamouni, whereas Wordsworth informs us that " he never visited the vale of Chamouni, or was near it in his life."

Upon the authority of De Quincey, it is stated that Coleridge founded the " Hymn to Chamouni " on a short poem upon the same subject, by Frederika Brun. " The mere framework of the poem is exactly the same," he says, " but the dry bones of the German outline have been created by Coleridge into the fulness of life."

Coleridge revealed his omnivorous appetite for reading in his early life, for he is reported to have " read straight through a circulating library, folios and all ; " and when in his fifteenth year, he says, " I had bewildered myself in metaphysics and theological controversy." The life-story of this gifted writer is a sad one to peruse, full of inconsistencies and errors ; and many of his misfortunes and sufferings were self-inflicted. If his resort to opium-eating was at first for the relief of his rheumatism, soon the remedy in his case became worse than the disease. How painful to read are his own confessions of his infatuated use of the pernicious drug. " In short, conceive whatever is most wretched, helpless, hopeless, and you will form as tolerable a notion of my state as it is possible for a good man to have!" Poor Coleridge ! his irresolution and indolence were like evil genii hovering over him through his whole life. In fine, he was a great genius with a great infirmity ; the twinhood of mental strength and feebleness, he claims at once our reverence and our deep compassion.

De Quincey informs us, when referring to Coleridge and his opium habit, that, like the poet, when his powers of composition for any length of time had been exerted, the result of his exertions produced a feeling of disgust. "And in after years," he states, "Coleridge confessed that he never could read anything he had written without a sense of overpowering disgust." Reverting to his own case, which was nearly the same as his, he continues :—

"At times when I had slept at more regular hours, for several nights consecutively, and had armed myself by a sudden increase of the opium for a few days running, I recovered, at times, a remarkable glow of jovial spirits. In some such artificial respites it was from my usual state of distress, and purchased at a heavy price of subsequent suffering, that I wrote the greater part of the *Opium Confessions.*" The narrative part preceding the incoherent dreams which that work describes " was written," he says, " with singular rapidity, but the dreams themselves were composed slowly, and by separate efforts of thought. These circumstances I mention to account for my having written anything in a happy or genial state of mind, when I was in a general state of mind so different by my own description."

Audubon, the ornithologist, who seems to have been a born naturalist, tells us that

"no roof seemed so secure to him as that formed of the dense foliage under which the feathered tribes were seen to resort, or the caves and fissures of the massy rocks to which the dark-winged cormorant and the curlew retired to rest, or to protect themselves from the fury of the tempest."

To advance his skill as a draughtsman he went to Paris, and studied under the celebrated artist David. Returning again to the New World, he revisited the woods and fields with increased ardour and enthusiasm ; he ransacked the prairies and mountains as well as streams and rivers to learn the habits and retreats of the feathered minstrels of the wilderness. His object at first was not to become a writer, but simply to indulge a passion, to enjoy the study of these beautiful creatures

of the air. It was Prince Lucien Bona-
parte, an accomplished naturalist, who
first incited him to arrange his beautiful
drawings in a form for publication. With
this object in view he revisited prairies,
lakes, rivers, and sea shore, and enriched
his portfolio with a mass of information
and a large number of drawings, when an
accident occurred to his collection. The
story is thus briefly given. Leaving his
home in Kentucky, he went to Philadelphia,
and placing his drawings carefully in a box
he gave them for safe keeping into the
charge of a relative. After an absence of
several months he returned, and on opening the box to his dismay he discovered,
instead of his thousand sketches and portraits, nothing remained to him but a pair
of Norway rats with their progeny nestled
among innumerable bits of paper. The
poor artist was overwhelmed; he slept not
for a few nights, but his courage returned,
and with a new resolution he again sallied
forth with notebook, pencil, and gun into
the woods as gaily as if nothing had happened. He said he might make better
drawings after all than those which had

been destroyed, and this he accomplished
within an interval of three years. In
reading Audubon's books you feel the
fresh air blowing in your face, scent the
odour of the prairie flowers and autumn
woods, or hear the surging of the sea.
He takes you into the squatter's hut, in
the lowly swamp, where the tells the story
of the woodcutter's pioneer life; or he
sallies out in the night to hunt the conger,
and when daylight returns he invokes the
fairy singers of the woods to your listening
ear. Audubon's life was full of romantic
adventure, and after encountering and
surmounting difficulties that would have
discouraged other adventurous spirits, he
took his splendid collection of drawings
to Europe. There he met with the cordial
friendship and aid of such men as Herschel,
Cuvier, Humboldt, Brewster, Wilson, and
Sir Walter Scott. His grand work forms
four large folio volumes, comprising four
hundred and forty-eight coloured pictures
of the birds of America, life-size ; each is
so faithfully portrayed that you catch an
idea of the bird's habits and nature as
well as its plumage. As a monument of

American devotion to ornithological science this stately work is unrivalled.

Alexander Wilson, of Paisley, was one in whose " heart the birds nestled and sang." He, like Audubon, acquired an undying fame by first making known to the world of science the feathered denizens of the American forests. In early manhood he went to America, and soon began his favourite pursuit in forming his collection of birds, as the basis of his work on American ornithology. He had the good fortune, as soon as he needed, to secure a willing publisher, and he found one in Bradford of Boston. In 1808 Wilson made an extended tour through the wilds and forests, and in little more than seven years, " without patronage, fortune, or recompense," he accomplished more than the combined body of naturalists of Europe had achieved in a century.

VI.

ROGERS. — BUTLER'S "HUDIBRAS." — SOUTHEY. — CRABBE. — FRANKLIN'S "AUTOBIOGRAPHY."—CHARLES LAMB. — BYRON. — MOORE. — CARLYLE. — POE.—DANA.—PRESCOTT.—HOOD.

ROGERS'S *Pleasures of Memory*, published in 1792, and written principally during his leisure moments in his banking house, had an immediate and astonishing success. His *Italy* proved less successful, and the author revised the poem and published an elegantly illustrated edition of the work, which for its artistic beauty surpassed anything then produced. The cost was enormous, but the poet was wealthy. His most approved production is generally thought to be his *Human Life*, which appeared in 1819. Mr. Rogers was offered the laureateship in 1850, but he declined the proffered honour on account of his advanced age. He was engaged on *The Pleasures of Memory* for nine years, on *Human Life* for nearly the same space of time, and *Italy* was not completed in less than sixteen years.

The remark was once made to Moore, the poet, that it was supposed his verses slipped off his tongue as if by magic, and a passage of great ease was quoted. "Why, sir," replied Moore, "that line cost me hours, days, and weeks of attrition before it would come."

Pope and Goldsmith were among the hard workers with their brains. Goldsmith considered four lines a day good work. He was seven years in "beating out the pure gold" of his *Deserted Village*.

Samuel Butler commenced his satirical poem *Hudibras* when engaged with one of Cromwell's generals, Sir Samuel Luke, a Bedfordshire gentleman, where he had an opportunity of studying the habits and characters of the Puritans, that personage having been the original of the "ever-memorable knight." The first three cantos of *Hudibras* were published in 1663, and

the poem became exceedingly popular
with the Court and cavalier party. Butler
seems to have received unbounded praise,
but no Court patronage followed, for he
died in abject poverty in 1680. The
original idea of *Hudibras* was derived from
Don Quixote, and although it is now
probably but little read, yet the witty
couplets and wise saws of *Hudibras* still
linger among the familiar sayings that
we are accustomed to use and to hear in
our social talk, without remembering
whence they have originated. –

It has been said of Butler that he was
no less remarkable for his poverty than
his pride. A friend of his one evening
invited him to supper, and contrived to
place in his pocket a purse containing one
hundred guineas. On his discovering this
good service of his friend, he hurried back
and returned the gift with expressions of
great displeasure at the supposed insult!
Butler was not a model of good behaviour
on many occasions, and to this infirmity
in part may be attributed his destitution
and neglect by society. Charles II.,
although he is said to have carried a copy

of *Hudibras* about with him in his pocket, does not seem ever to have put anything into the pocket or purse of its author.

Southey, in a letter to a friend, thus describes his average day's work :—

"Three pages of history (of Portugal) after breakfast, then to transcribe and copy for the press, or make selections and biographies (for *Specimens of the British Poets*), or what else suits my humour till dinner-time. After dinner, I read, write letters, see the newspapers, and very often indulge in a siesta. After tea I go to poetry (the *Curse of Kehama*) and correct and re-write, and copy till I am tired ; and then turn to anything else till supper. And this is my life."

He was never so happy as when he sat among his books, pen in hand, adding newly written sheets to the pile of manuscripts already in his table drawer. His incessant toil brought on the sad calamity of a brain worn out, and caused the busy workman to wander among the books he had gathered around him and yet loved although the light of reason had passed into eclipse.

Southey, one of the most prolific of poets, is said to have destroyed more verses written between his twentieth and thirtieth years, than he published during his whole life. It is a sad fact to add that for nearly three years he may be said to have survived himself; he used to sit in his library, in hopeless vacuity of mind, unable to hold further converse with his books, which he so loved, as we well know from his tributary stanzas :—

" My days among the dead are passed ! around me
   I behold
Where'er these casual eyes are cast, the mighty
   minds of old ;
      My never-failing friends are they,
      With whom I converse night and day.
With them I take delight in weal, and seek relief
   in woe ;
And, while I understand and feel how much to
   them I owe,
      My cheeks have often been bedewed
      With tears of thoughtful gratitude."

Of Franklin's *Autobiography* the first part was written at Twyford, England, in 1771, while he was visiting Shipley, Bishop of St. Asaph. This portion ended with Franklin's marriage in 1730. In 1784 he resumed work on the second part of his memoirs while living at Passy, near Paris. When thus engaged he had not with him his first part, and supposed it had been left at his home in Philadelphia, after his return from England in 1775. The third part was begun in 1788, while Franklin was in Philadelphia, and is brought down to 1757. This portion ends the *Autobiography* as it has been usually printed, except in the edition of Mr. John Bigelow, in 1868, which includes a fourth part consisting of a few pages written in 1789, and not to be found elsewhere in English. These are rather of a political character, and bring the memoirs down a year later, when they close. Immediately after Dr. Franklin's death, in 1790, the first portion was published in French in Paris,—a remarkable fact, that a work destined to have so great popularity should first appear in a foreign tongue. It is, in fact, an English translation from a French translation of the original English !

Franklin tells us that from his earliest days he was passionately fond of reading, and that " all the money that came into his hands was laid out in the purchase of books." Among his first acquisitions were Bunyan's works, Plutarch's *Lives*, Defoe's

Essay on Projects, and Mather's *Essay to do Good.* The two last, he adds, gave him "a turn of thinking, that had an influence on some of the principal future events of my life."

Crabbe's poems, comprising *The Village* and *The Library,* were so much admired in manuscript by Edmund Burke, that he took them to Dodsley, who published them in a volume. Burke befriended the poet in many ways, and was the means of his being appointed to positions of ecclesiastical preferment. Crabbe subsequently produced *The Borough* and *Tales of the Hall,* works which brought him into friendship with Southey, Wordsworth, Campbell, Moore, Irving, and Sir Walter Scott ; and it may be added the last books the great novelist called for during his last days were the Bible and Crabbe's poems.

Charles Lamb's life record is, indeed, a sad one. Who has not been made familiar with the details of its terrible trials and its heroic self-negation ? Is it any wonder that his writings were desultory and fragmentary, broken, as one may say, like the life out of which they struggled?

The wonder is not that he wrote as he did, but that he wrote at all. His strongest, if not his chief, incentive to literature was the necessity for earning money in order to maintain his poor mad sister,—for mad she continued at intervals all her life, and was conscious of the dreadful fact. So conscious, indeed, that when she felt her reason giving way, she and Charles used to walk to the mad-house together, hand-in-hand, weeping as if their hearts would break![1]

"The adoption of the signature ' Elia ' by Charles Lamb," says Talfourd, " was purely acci- dental. His first contribution was a description of the Old South Sea House, where Lamb had passed a few months' novitiate as a clerk, thirty years before, and of its inmates, who had long passed away ; and, remembering the name of a gay, light-hearted foreigner, who had fluttered there at that time, he subscribed his name to the essay," instead of his own.

The *Essays of Elia* are unique in litera- ture ; they are a reflex of the author's peculiar humour, whims, poetic instinct, and his kindly nature.

It is remarkable that Charles Lamb

[1] R. H. Stoddard.

should have enjoyed the friendship of such opposite characters during his life as Wordsworth, Southey, and Coleridge. We do not know what circumstances originated his writings, but it is pleasant to know that before his literary productions attracted the applause of the world, he had a select circle of contemporaries who could appreciate them. Some writers have been compared to musical glasses, because you can get no music out of them until they are *wetted.* You may have seen a portrait of Lamb that is suggestive of this fact; his " particular wanity " having been gin and water. Byron, Moore, Campbell, and others, might be named as of the class. Charles Lamb had another infirmity, which was, however, an involuntary one, an impediment in his speech, or, as he once expressed it, " gifted with a stutter, or catapult, for it shot words out of his mouth." Although accustomed to it all his life, he was naturally annoyed if any one noticed it openly. On one occasion, among the guests at Moxon the publisher's there was a gentleman whose wife made herself prominently unpleasant by her loud and incessant talking, and by the shrewishness of her temper, her husband being the chief sufferer. After a short remark from Lamb, the gentleman observed to him, " I am sorry to perceive that you have an *impediment* in your speech, sir." "Yes, sir, I have," replied Lamb,— "don't you wish that your wife had ? "

Like Thomson, Lamb does not seem to have been an early riser, as we gather from his paper about " Rising with the Lark," which reads in this wise :—

" At what precise minute that little airy musician doffs his night gear, and prepares to tune up his unseasonable matins, we are not naturalist enough to determine. But for a mere human gentleman—that has no orchestra business to call him from his warm bed to such preposterous exercises—we take ten, or half after ten (eleven, of course, during this Christmas solstice) to be the very earliest hour at which he can begin to think of abandoning his pillow. To *think* of it, we say ; for to do it in earnest requires another half-hour's good consideration."

A clever limner thus sketches our famed essayist :—

" A small spare man, close gaitered to the knee,
    In suit of rusty black whose folds betray

The last loved dusty folio, bought to-day,
And carried proudly to the sanctuary
Of home (and Mary's) keeping.

                  Quaintly wise
In saws and knowledge of a bygone age,
Each Old World fancy on a yellow page,
Tracked by the 'smoky-brightness' of his eyes,
Shone new-illumined ; or in daring flight
That outvied Ariel, his spirit caught
The reflex of a rainbowed cloud, and taught
The glories of a Dreamland of delight ! " [1]

Byron has told us that the *Giaour* is but a string of passages.

" This accusation, brought by himself, against his poems is not just, but when the author goes on to say of them that 'their faults, whatever they may be, are those of negligence and not of labour,' he says what is perfectly true. *Lara* he declares he 'wrote while undressing after coming home from balls and masquerades, in the year of revelry 1814.' The *Bride of Abydos* was written in four, the *Corsair* in ten days. He calls this 'a humiliating confession, as it proves my own want of judgment in publishing, and the public's in reading, things which cannot have stamina for permanency.' Again he does his poems injustice ; the producer of such poems could not but publish them, the public could not but read them. Nor could Byron have produced

---

[1] *Temple Bar.*

his work in any other fashion ; his poetic work could not have first grown and matured in his own mind, and then come forth as an organic whole. Byron had not enough of the artist in him for this, nor enough of self-command. He wrote, as he truly tells us, to relieve himself, and he went on writing because he found the relief became indispensable. But it was inevitable that works so produced should be, in general, 'a string of passages,' poured out, as he describes them, with rapidity and excitement, and with new passages constantly suggesting themselves, and added while his work was going through the press. But Byron has a wonderful power of vividly conceiving a single incident, a single situation,—of throwing himself upon it, grasping it as if it were real and he saw it and felt it, and of making us see and feel it too. To the poetry of Byron the world has ardently paid homage ; full justice from his contemporaries, perhaps even more than justice, his torrent of poetry received. His poetry was admired, adored, 'with all its imperfections on its head,' in spite of negligence, in spite of diffuseness, in spite of repetitions, in spite of whatever faults it possessed. His name is still great and brilliant."[1]

Scott lavished extravagant praise on Byron, comparing him for versatility and poetic power to Shakespeare, while others say " he has treated hardly any subject but

[1] Matthew Arnold.

one—himself." Truth lies between the extremes.

Lord Byron wrote his poem *The Prisoner of Chillon* in 1816, shortly after he left England for the last time, and while he was living with Shelley at a little inn at Morges, two miles from Lausanne in Switzerland. When he composed his poem, he did not know that there had been a *real* prisoner of Chillon : it was the mere sight of the dungeon that suggested the tragedy to his imagination. When Byron was informed of the fact of there having been an actual captive—the illustrious Bonnivard—incarcerated there, he wrote the fine apostrophe to his memory.

Bonnivard was a Swiss patriot, whose imprisonment has made this castle on the eastern shore of the Lake of Geneva one of the shrines of freedom. Bonnivard, when but sixteen years old, inherited from his uncle the rich priory of St. Victor ; but having espoused the cause of the city of Geneva against Charles V. of Savoy, the latter sequestered his estates and imprisoned him. After two years he regained his liberty, and again took up arms for the recovery of his estates, but was again defeated, and confined in the castle of Chillon for six years, when at the Reformation he was liberated.

As to the sources of Byron's several productions, it may be said of them, as of his *Childe Harold*, which is supposed to be largely autobiographic, that they owe their existence to the moods and modes of his own experience and life, as well as the incidents and characters he met with in his travels.

It has been suggested that there is a marked resemblance between the career of Shelley and that of Byron. Both were descended from ancient families. Both of them were educated in the conservative atmosphere of public schools and universities—Byron at Harrow and Cambridge, Shelley at Eton and Oxford. Both of them were trained under conditions which were wholly opposed to the adoption of radical principles. Both of them were married at a comparatively early age, and both of them soon separated from their wives. Both of them were remarkable for their reckless disregard of public opinion, and for the license with which they attacked every political, social, and religious institution. Shelley, it is said, caught inspiration for his muse as he wandered amid the classic ruins of the Palace of the Cæsars and other historic sites, as Byron did loitering among the columns and galleries of the Coliseum. Shelley, indeed, tells us that *The Prometheus* was written upon the mountainous ruins of the Baths of Caracalla, among the flowery glades and thickets of odoriferous perfume. The bright blue sky of Rome, and the effect of the vigorous awakening of spring in that divinest of climates, and the new life with which it drenches the spirits even to intoxication, were the inspiration of this drama. Shelley while an Oxford student was a voracious reader; he read at all times,—even while walking the streets and when a-bed.

One of Moore's descriptive poems was written when the poet visited Norfolk in Virginia. It is founded upon the following legend :—

" A young man who lost his mind,—said to have been occasioned by the death of a beautiful maiden whom he loved,—suddenly disappearing from his friends, was never afterwards heard of. As he had frequently been heard to say that the girl was not dead, but gone to the ' Dismal Swamp,' it was believed that he had wandered into that dreary wilderness, and had perished among its forest of foliage, or its dreadful morasses."

"They made her a grave too cold and damp for a
 soul so warm and true ;
And she's gone to the ' Lake of the Dismal Swamp,'
 where, all night long, by a fire-fly lamp,
  She paddles her white canoe ! "

Moore also, during his passage of the St. Lawrence from Kingston, pencilled the lines (nearly as they stand in his works) of the *Canadian Boat-song* in the blank page of a book which he happened to have in his canoe.

The poet wrote his famous *Lalla Rookh* in his cottage near Dovedale, where he also composed many of his beautiful songs and melodies. Concerning this poem, in which the reader is transported to the palaces of Delhi and the gardens of Cashmere, the author tells us that he never reached to the height of his own conception until the thought occurred to him of embodying in his work the per.

secuted race of the Ghebers or fire-worshippers, who, like the Irish, had long suffered oppression.

For brevity of stature Nature seems to have more than compensated the poet with high intellect, and this is evinced in the splendour of his imagery and the Oriental magnificence of his Oriental romances. It was once the privilege of the writer to meet together the two representative bards, Moore and Campbell,—two " bright particular stars " of the first magnitude. The one has sung to us of the gentle passion in mellifluous strains, and the other has given us bright visions of the *Pleasures of Hope*, of which poem a brother-bard has said : " Whether taken as a whole or in parts, it is to be preferred to any didactic poem of equal length in the English language." Campbell wrote it at Edinburgh, when he was but twenty-one years old, and so prolonged was its popularity that it ultimately brought to its author four thousand five hundred pounds.

" Coming home to my house one evening, in Park Square, where, as usual, the poet had dropped in to spend a quiet hour," writes his biographer, " I told him that I had been agreeably detained listening to some street music, near Portman Square. 'Vocal or instrumental?' he enquired. 'Vocal,' I replied ; 'the song was an old favourite, remarkably good, and of at least forty years' standing.' 'Ha!' said he, 'I congratulate the author, whoever he is.' 'And so do I,' I responded ; 'it was your own song, 'The Soldier's Dream.'"

Carlyle was " an indomitable worker from first to last." "One monster there is in the world," he says,—" the idle man." He did not merely preach the gospel of work ; he was it Each of his review articles cost him a month or more of serious work. *Sartor Resartus* cost him nine months, the *French Revolution* three years, *Cromwell* four years, *Frederick the Great* thirteen years. In *Past and Present*, Carlyle has unconsciously painted his own life and character in truer colours than has any one else.

" His books are not easy reading ; they are a kind of wrestling to most persons. His style is like a road made of rocks ; when it is good there is nothing like it ; and when it is bad, there is nothing like it. During his last great work,—the thirteen years spent in his study at the top of his house, writing the history of Frederick,—this isolation, this incessant toil and penitential gloom, were such as only religious devotees have voluntarily imposed upon themselves. A sort of anthropomorphic greed and hunger possessed him always, an insatiable craving for strong, picturesque characters, and for contact and conflict with them. This was his ruling passion (and it amounted to a passion) all his days. He fed his soul on heroes and heroic qualities, and all his literary exploits were a search for these things."[1]

The *French Revolution* is generally considered to be Carlyle's greatest production ; but when he had written his last paragraph, the author said :—

" What they will do with this book none knows, but they have not had for two hundred years any book that came more truly from a man's very heart, and so let them trample it under foot and hoof, as they see best."

But its great merits were not discovered until the publication of his *Cromwell* brought to him popularity and fame for both works. It has been said of his *History of the French Revolution* that—

"No mere industry, nothing but native genius, could have enabled him to see the past as he did, to behold the actors as they lived and suffered, to

[1] Burroughs, *Fresh Fields.*

make all the crowded scene visible to every spectator, and construct the whole into a prose epic,
full of humour, full of tragedy, as true though not
as musical as the *Iliad.*"[1]

Carlyle has been not inaptly called " the
Censor of the Age;" his criticisms were
often harsh and severe, yet he was an
astute and trenchant critic.   Amidst much
laudation from the highest literary sources,
he yet was the subject of strictures of an
opposite kind; for instance, we are con-
fronted with the following question, proposed even by an eminent Scotch critic:—

" Can any living man point to a single practical
passage in any of his volumes? If not, what is
the real value of Mr. Carlyle's writings? What is
Mr. Carlyle himself but a phantasm of the species
he is pleased to denounce?"

We shall see by his writings.

One of the most eloquent pieces of
word-painting which we have seen from
any English writer is the following extract
from Carlyle's *Sartor Resartus :—*

" 'I look down into all that wasp-nest or bee-
hive,' have we heard him say, 'and witness their

[1] *Fraser's Magazine.*

wax-laying, and honey-making, and poison-brewing, and choking by sulphur. From the palace esplanade, where music plays while His Serene Highness is pleased to eat his victuals, down to the low lane, where, in her door-sill the aged widow, knitting for a thin livelihood, sits to feel the afternoon sun. I see it all; for, except the Schlosskirche weathercock, no biped stands so high. Couriers arrive bestrapped and bebooted, bearing joy and sorrow bagged-up in pouches of leather; there, top-laden and with four swift horses, rolls in the country Baron and his household; here, on timber-leg, the lamed soldier hops painfully along, begging alms; a thousand carriages and wains and cars come tumbling in with food, with young Rusticity and other raw produce, animate or inanimate, and go tumbling out again with produce manufactured. That living flood, pouring through these streets, of all qualities and ages, knowest thou whence it is coming, whither it is going? *Aus der Ewigkeit zu der Ewigkeit hin,*—from Eternity, onwards to Eternity! These are apparitions,—what else? Are they not souls rendered visible: in bodies, that took shape, and will lose it, melting into air? Their solid pavement is a picture of the sense; they walk on the bosom of nothing, blank Time is behind them and before them. Or fanciest thou, the red and yellow clothes-screen yonder, with spurs on its heels and feather in its crown, is but of to-day, without a yesterday or to-morrow; and had not rather its Ancestor alive when Hengist and Horsa overran thy island? Friend, thou seest here a living link in that tissue of History, which inweaves all being : watch well, or it will be past thee, and seen no more."

" One day the talk fell upon his books. ' Poor old *Sartor!* ' he said. ' It's a book in which I take little satisfaction ; really a book worth very little as a work of art,—a fragmentary, disjointed, vehement production. It was written when I was livin' at Craigenputtock, one o' the solitariest places on the face o' the earth ; a wild moorland place where one might lead a wholesome, simple life, and might labour without interruption, and be not altogether without peace such as London cannot give. We were quite alone, and there is much that is beautiful and precious in them as I look back on those days.' He went on to tell of the difficulties he had in getting the book published, of which an account has since been given in his *Life*, and of the lack of favour with which it was at first received, and then he said : ' But it's been so with all my books. I've had little satisfaction or encouragement in the doin' of them, and the most satisfaction I can get out of them now is the sense of havin' shouldered a heavy burden o' work, an' not flinched under it. I've had but one thing to say from beginnin' to end o' them, and that was that there's no other reliance for this world or any other but just the Truth, and that if men did not want to be damned to all eternity, they had best give up lyin' and all kinds o' falsehood ; that the world was far gone already through lyin', and that there's no hope for it save just so far as men find out and believe the Truth, and match their lives to it."[1]

"*Ach, mein Lieber*," said he once, at midnight, when we had returned from the coffee house in rather earnest talk, " it is a true sublimity to dwell here.   These fringes of lamp-light, struggling up through smoke and thousandfold exhalation, some fathoms into the ancient reign of Night, what thinks Bootes of them, as he leads his hunting-dogs over the Zenith in their leash of sidereal fire? That stifled hum of Midnight, when traffic has lain down to rest; and the chariot wheels of Vanity still rolling here and there through distant streets, are bearing her to Halls roofed-in, and lighted to the due pitch for her; and only vice and misery, to prowl or to moan like night-birds, are abroad ; that hum, I say, like the stertorous, unquiet slumber of sick life, is heard in Heaven !   Oh, under that hideous coverlet of vapours and putre-factions and unimaginable gases, what a ferment-ing vat lies simmering and hid !   The joyful and the sorrowful are there ; men are dying there, men are being born, men are praying—on the other side of a brick partition, men are cursing ; and around them all is the vast, void Night. The proud grandee still lingers in his perfumed saloons, or reposes within damask curtains ; wretchedness cowers into truckle-beds, or shivers, hunger-stricken, nto its lair of straw ; in obscure cellars, *rouge-et-*

[1] C. E. Norton.

noir languidly emits its voice-of-destiny to haggard hungry villains ; while councillors of state sit plotting and playing their high chess game, whereof the pawns are men. The lover whispers his mistress that the coach is ready ; and she, full of hope and fear, glides down to fly with him over the borders; the thief, still more silently, sets to his picklocks and crowbars, or lurks in wait till the watchmen first snore in their boxes. Gay mansions, with supper-rooms and dancing-rooms, are full of light and music, and high-swelling hearts ; but, in the condemned cells, the pulse of life beats tremulous and faint, and blood-shot eyes look out through the darkness."

Carlyle's knowledge of the German language was such as to place him in advance of any of his contemporaries, and this caused him to be styled a literary Columbus, since he opened up to the English reader the then unknown world of German thought. And it will not be forgotten that to Carlyle has been reserved the great honour of replacing in the pantheon of English history the statue of England's greatest ruler.

We are all familiar with Poe's remarkable rhythmic poem, "The Raven," but we may not be so well acquainted with its origin or its author. "When he died," in

1849, wrote his biographer, "literary art lost one of its most brilliant, but erratic stars." He was at all times a dreamer, dwelling in ideal' realms, peopled with the creatures and the accidents of his brain. The poem of "The Raven" was probably much more nearly than has been supposed a reflection and an echo of his own history. *He* was that bird's—

. . . "Unhappy master, when unmerciful Disaster
Followed fast and followed faster, till his songs one
    burden bore—
Till the dirges of his Hope that melancholy burden
    bore
             Of never—never more!"

This remarkable poem was written, it is stated, under very afflictive circumstances, while the poet's wife was rapidly wasting away with consumption at his humble cottage at Bloomingdale, New York. It was a spontaneous inspiration of the surroundings at the time.

Among earlier American bards we instance Drake, whose imaginative poem, "The Culprit Fay," so replete with poetic beauty, is a fairy tale of the highlands of the Hudson. The origin of the poem is traced to a conversation with Cooper the novelist, and Fitz-Greene Halleck the poet, who, speaking of the Scottish streams and their legendary associations, insisted that the American rivers were not susceptible of like poetic treatment. Drake thought otherwise, and to make his position good, produced three days after this poem.

Of the poems of William C. Bryant, perhaps that best known is his "Thanatopsis," written when he was in his nineteenth year, and first printed in the *North American Review* for 1817, although only about half of the poem as we now have it was then given. Like the familiar poems of Longfellow, this early production, with others, of Bryant will become classic.

One of the most eminent of American historical writers, W. H. Prescott, when young, met with an accident which greatly impaired his eyesight ; but, notwithstanding this difficulty, with the aid of a noctograph he devoted himself to historical studies. His first work was his *History of the Reign of Ferdinand and Isabella*, which occupied him twelve years, and was published in 1838. This work at once established his reputation as one of the foremost of living historians.

J. Fenimore Cooper published in 1821 *The Spy*, a novel founded on an incident said to have happened in the great war of American independence. Few first works of an author have been equally successful, either in America or England. It exhibited to the reader new characters and scenes, depicted with great clearness and picturesque effect. Cooper produced a succession of somewhat similar works for nearly thirty years, until his death in 1851. His *Last of the Mohicans* has been considered his masterpiece.

Every person has, it is presumed, read or heard of Mrs. Stowe's *Uncle Tom's Cabin*, and it is only necessary to refer to its origin. It was commenced in 1851, as a serial story of southern slave-life, in the *National Era* of Washington. When completed in 1852, it was published at Boston in book form, and its popularity was so prodigious, both in England and the United States, that over a million copies were sold, and many translations also were published in Europe.

Of the personal history of that poet of the people, Tom Hood, whose memory, it has been said, is "emblazoned with a halo of light-hearted mirth and pleasantry," we do not know so much as we desire. Yet we may gather something of his genial nature from the deep human sympathies which characterise many of his productions. If he was "the prince of punsters," he was no less the poet of pathos. Of Hood it may be said that he literally " learned in suffering what he taught in song," for his whole life seems to have been a lingering sickness. Referring to his own physical debility, he thus writes :—

"That man who has never known a day's illness is a moral dunce, one who has lost the greatest moral lesson in life,—who has skipped the finest lecture in that great school of humanity, the sick chamber. Let him be versed in metaphysics, profound in mathematics, a ripe scholar in the classics, a bachelor of arts, or even a doctor in divinity, yet he is one of those gentlemen whose education has been neglected. For all his college acquirements, how inferior he is in wholesome knowledge to the mortal who has had a quarter's gout, or a half year of ague ; how infinitely below the fellow-creature who has been soundly taught his tic-douloureux, thoroughly grounded in rheumatism, and deeply *red* in the scarlet fever ! "

" There were scarcely any events in the life of Thomas Hood ; but one condition there was of too potent determining importance, --life-long ill-health ; and one circumstance of moment,—a commercial failure, and consequent expatriation. Beyond this, little presents itself for record in the outward facts of his upright and beneficial career, bright with genius and corruscating with wit, dark with the lengthening and deepening shadow of death."

In 1826 Hood published his first series of *Whims and Oddities*; the volume that followed contained " The Plea for the Midsummer Fairies," and " Hero and Leander," with some others. In 1829 appeared one of the most famous of all Hood's poems of a narrative character, " The Dream of Eugene Aram." Equally a master in the comic and the tragic muse, he has alike charmed us with his touching pathos as with his wit and humour. His " boundlessly whimsical idiosyncrasy " was doubtless born with him ; but it is supposed its development may be traced, in part at least, to his early reading of *Humphrey Clinker*, *Tristram Shandy*, *Tom Jones*, and other works of that period. In 1841 Hood succeeded Theodore Hook in the editorship of the *New Monthly Magazine*. Hood's poems are all good, but among his most famous may be named, " The Plea for the Midsummer Fairies," " The Dream of Eugene Aram," " The Bridge of Sighs," " The Haunted House," and " The Song of the Shirt," which last was written in one evening, and came out anonymously in the Christmas number of *Punch* for 1843; " it ran like wildfire, and rang like a tocsin through the land." And yet, when he wrote it, he thought so little of its merit that he was about to throw it into the waste-basket, but was prevented by his wife, who told him it was the best thing he had written. The world has endorsed her verdict, and, on his monument in Kensal Green Cemetery, are the words inscribed, " He sang the 'Song of the Shirt.'" The editor of *Punch*, looking over his letters one morning, opened an envelope inclosing a poem which the writer said had been rejected by three London journals. He begged the editor to consign it to the waste-paper basket if it was not thought suitable for *Punch*, as the author was " sick of the sight of it." The poem was signed " Tom Hood," and was entitled " The Song of the Shirt."

It was submitted to the weekly meeting of the editor and principal contributors, several of whom opposed its publication as unsuitable to the pages of a comic journal. Mr. Lemon, however, was so firmly impressed with its beauty that he published it.

VII.

MRS. BROWNING.—WASHINGTON IRVING.
— HAWTHORNE. — LONGFELLOW. —
HOLMES.—WHITTIER.—TENNYSON.

THE life-story of the gifted au
thoress Mrs. Elizabeth Barrett
Browning is as touchingly interesting as it is romantic. When only
sixteen years old, she published her " Essay
on Mind and other Poems ;" ten years
later she became an invalid by the rupture
of a blood-vessel ; this necessitated her
removal from London to the sea coast.
Her brother, with other relatives, accompanied her to Torquay, and *there* occurred
the fatal event which saddened her youth,
and gave to her poetry a deeper hue of
thought and devotional feeling. One
summer morning her brother, with two
young friends, embarked on board a small
sailing-vessel ; they were all said to be

good sailors and familiar with the coast, and yet but a few minutes after leaving shore, and in sight of their very windows, as they were crossing the bar, the boat went down, and all who were in her perished ! Even the bodies were never recovered. This sad event nearly killed poor Elizabeth Barrett, for she was haunted with the feeling that she had been in some way the cause of the terrible tragedy. Still, she clung to her literary pursuits, finding relief from suffering and diversion from the painful memory in her muse. On her return to her home in London her life for many years was that of a confirmed and seemingly hopeless invalid. Virtually exiled from society, for she saw but few friends, her silent companions were a Hebrew Bible, many Greek writers with Plato at their head, and no small range of polyglot reading. Thus the long and dreary hours of her illness were soothed by composition and study, even of authors of abstruse and profound learning. In 1844 the first collected edition of her poems was published, in two volumes In this edition appeared for the first time " Lady Geraldine's Courtship," one of her most popular poems, and yet written by her, it is stated, in the incredibly brief space of twelve hours ! After her recovery to comparative health, and her somewhat romantic marriage with Mr. Robert Browning, her residence was at Florence, where it continued to be for about fourteen years. It was here, in 1851, she produced the poem called, after her Italian home, " Casa Guidi Windows," devoted to the political affairs of Italy ; and five years later appeared her beautiful narrative poem, in nine books, which she named " Aurora Leigh," a series of romantic sketches of modern English life and characters.

" One or two of her poems may be indicated, as ' The Cry of the Children,' which for pathos may take rank with Hood's ' Song of the Shirt,' and her fine poem, ' Aurora Leigh,' which, being more natural or less metaphysical, has made its appeal more successfully to the common heart. Her ' Lady Geraldine's Courtship,' also, at once became popular, and deservedly so, for it is a charming poem, although it was the product of only about twelve hours. Her life-story is a shaded one until her union with the poet Browning, when married relations seemed to inspire her with new ambition, as well as happiness. Her cloister-life of maidenhood in England was at an end ; fifteen happy and illustrious years in Italy lay before her ; and in her case the proverb, *Cælum non animum*, was unfulfilled. Never was there a more complete transmutation of the habits and sympathies of life than that which she experienced beneath the blue Italian skies. Still, before all and above all, her refined soul remained in allegiance to the eternal muse." [1]

Washington Irving and Wilkie the painter were fellow-travellers on the Continent, about the year 1827. In their rambles about some of the old cities of Spain they were more than once struck with scenes and incidents which reminded them of passages in the *Arabian Nights Entertainments.* The painter urged Irving to write something that should illustrate those peculiarities, "something in the Haroun-al-Raschid style," which should have much of that Arabian spice which pervades everything in Spain. The author set to work *con amore*, and produced two goodly volumes of Arabesque sketches and tales, founded on popular traditions

[1] Stedman's *Victorian Poets.*

and legends. Irving's study was an apartment assigned to him, by privilege, in the Alhambra itself, by the courtesy of the Governor. Wilkie had to leave for London soon after, but Irving remained for several months spell-bound in the enchanted building.

"How many legends," wrote he, "and traditions, true and fabulous,—how many songs and romances, Spanish and Arabian, of love, and war, and chivalry, are associated with this old historic pile. It was my endeavour scrupulously to depict its half Spanish, half Oriental character, its mixture of the heroic, the poetic, and the grotesque,—to revive the traces of grace and beauty fast fading from its walls, to record the regal and chivalrous traditions concerning those who once trod its courts, and the whimsical and superstitious legends of the motley race now burrowing among its ruins."

In one of his letters Irving thus refers to his love for Spanish legendary lore :—

"They have a charm for me, having so much that is high-minded and chivalrous, and quaint, picturesque, and adventurous, and at times half comic about them."

Mr. Irving, when in Spain, delighted to run over the courts of the Alhambra and pick up fragments of legendary literature connected with the chivalry of Castile and Toledo. When at Madrid, and engaged on his *Life of Columbus*, he used to write from twelve to fourteen hours a day ; and, to use his own words :—

> "He never found outside of the walls of his study, any enjoyment equal to sitting at his writing desk."

Wrote Irving in one of his charming letters from Madrid :—

> "I pass most of my mornings in the library of the Jesuits' College of St. Isidoro. You cannot think what a delight I feel in passing through its galleries filled with old, parchment-bound books. It is a perfect wilderness of curiosity to me. What a deep-felt quiet luxury there is in delving into the rich ore of these old, neglected volumes. How these hours of uninterrupted intellectual enjoyment, so tranquil and independent, repay one for the *ennui* and disappointment too often experienced in the intercourse of society !"

In the author's "Apology" to his *Knickerbocker's History of New York* we read that this famous production originated in the idea of satirising a small handbook, which had then just appeared, entitled *A Picture of New York*.

" Like that, our work,' writes Mr. Irving, "was to begin with an historical sketch ; to be followed by notices of the customs, manners, and institutions of the city; written in a serio-comic vein, and treating local errors, follies, and abuses with good-natured satire. To burlesque the pedantic lore displayed in certain American works, our historical sketch was to commence with the creation of the world ; and we laid all kinds of works under contribution for trite citations, relevant or irrelevant, to give it the proper air of learned research. Before this crude mass of mock erudition could be digested into form, my brother departed for Europe, and I was left to prosecute the enterprise alone. I now altered the plan of the work : discarding all idea of a parody on the *Picture of New York*, I determined that what had been originally intended as an introductory sketch, should comprise the whole work, and form a comic history of the city. I accordingly moulded the mass of citations and disquisitions into introductory chapters, forming the first books; but it soon became evident to me, that, like Robinson Crusoe with his boat, I had begun on too large a scale, and that, to launch my history successfully, I must reduce its proportions. I accordingly resolved to confine it to the period of the Dutch domination, which, in its rise, progress, and decline, presented that unity of subject required by classic rule. This, then, broke upon me as the poetic age of our city,—poetic from its very obscurity ; and open, like the early and obscure days of ancient Rome, to all the embellishments of heroic fiction."

Of Irving's inimitable *Sketch Book* little need be said, except that the papers it comprises were, with two exceptions, written in England. These papers or *essays* were issued in serial form at first, and afterwards collected into two volumes. The critical acumen of the publishers was, however, sadly at fault, for until Scott interfered in their behalf, they awaited some agent to introduce them to the public. Mr. Murray, however, was wise and shrewd enough to do this service, greatly to the success of the work and the satisfaction of the author and himself.

It is a point on which professional writers are far from agreeing as to how far one must depend upon " moods " for doing the best literary work. No writer was a greater slave to moods than Washington Irving, who confessed his inability to do justice to himself, or to any subject, except when he " felt like it." When he was once at work he hardly gave himself time for rest and refreshment until the task before him was completed, or, as he said, until his "brain was wrung dry." His *Bracebridge Hall* was written in a mood, however, that lasted six weeks.

Mr. Irving's poetic temperament and love of romance found scope for their display in the chapters of his *Sketch Book* entitled " Rip Van Winkle," "The Spectre Bridegroom," and " The Legend of Sleepy Hollow." These were suggested to their author by the legendary lore of the Rhine and the Hartz Mountains. His own words sufficiently evince his fondness for adventure and travel; hence the character of his sketches of subjects quaint and somewhat unsought by other writers. He says :—

" I was always fond of visiting new scenes, and observing strange characters and manners. I made myself familiar with places famous in history or fable. I had beside this a desire to see the great men of the earth, and it has been my lot to have my roving passion gratified."

Referring, on one occasion, to the success of his *Sketch Book*, Irving said :—

" The writing of those stories was so unlike an inspiration, so utterly without any feeling of confidence which could be prophetic of their popularity."

Walking with his brother one dull day

over Westminster Bridge, he got to telling
the old Dutch stories which he had heard
at Tarrytown in his youth, when the
thought suddenly struck him,—I'll make
a memoranda of these for a book.
Leaving his brother soon after, he went
back to his lodgings, and jotted down
all the data ; and the next day—in
one of the darkest of London fogs—he
wrote out his "Legend of Sleepy
Hollow."

The paucity of data which confronts
us concerning the inception or origin of
many notable books may, doubtless, be
accounted for, to some extent at least,
by the fact that when their authors commenced to write them they either did not
think it worth while to put upon record
the circumstances that prompted or suggested them to write, or else they did not,
at the outset, foresee the proportions to
which their work was destined to attain,
—"they builded better than they knew."
It is also to be remembered that many
works of celebrity have been the result,
or rather the embodiment, of papers or
essays that had previously been published

in the serial or periodical form, as in the well-known instances of Dickens and Thackeray, as well as of Hawthorne, and many others. The last named had, like the others referred to, attained to great popularity as a writer in the literary magazines, before he collected his fugitive contributions into volumes. Of his *Twice-told Tales* the author himself wrote :—

> " The sketches are not, it is hardly necessary to say, profound ; but it is rather more remarkable that they so seldom, if ever, show any design on the writer's part to make them so."

The thoughtful reader of these volumes will scarcely acquiesce, however, with this modest estimate of them. Of all Hawthorne's productions, his most dramatic and popular book is, doubtless, *The Scarlet Letter.* In the author's introduction to the work, the reader will find a detailed account of the discovery of the " scarlet letter " in an upper apartment of the Salem Custom House, among heaps of old musty documents and manuscripts of various kinds, and some of a personal kind.

" But the object that most drew my attention was a mysterious package of fine red cloth, much worn and faded. There were traces about it of gold embroidery, wrought with wonderful skill ; and on it was the letter **A**. In the absorbing contemplation of the scarlet letter, I had hitherto neglected to examine a small roll of dingy paper, around which it had been twisted. This I now opened, and had the satisfaction to find, recorded by the old surveyor's pen, a reasonably complete explanation of the whole affair."

Plausible as reads this statement, there is said to be no reality in it, but that it is simply the product of the author's brain. When, during 1858, he visited Italy, he wrote *The Marble Fawn*, while residing in a spacious antique house in Florence. While Hawthorne was disgusted with Rome, he seems to have been enchanted with Florence, her memories and art-treasures. But to return to *The Scarlet Letter*, and here we cite from Mr. Field, his publisher :—

" In the winter of 1849, after he had been ejected from the Custom House, I went down to Salem to see him and inquire after his health. He was then living in a modest wooden house ; and we fell into talk about his future prospects, and he was, as I feared I should find him, in a very desponding mood."

He seemed to give up the hope of succeeding as a writer; but when his visitor was in the act of leaving, he handed to him a roll of manuscript, requesting him to take it to Boston, and examine and report upon it; adding, " It is either very good or very bad, I don't know which."

" ' On my way back to Boston,' says Mr. Field, ' I read the germ of *The Scarlet Letter* ; and before I slept that night I wrote him a note all aglow with admiration of the marvellous story he had put into my hands, and told him that I would come again into Salem the next day and arrange for its publication. Hawthorne seemed to think I was beside myself, and laughed sadly at my enthusiasm.' "

He went on with the book and finished it ; and in a letter to another friend,—

" I finished my book only yesterday ; one end being in the press at Boston, while the other was in my head here at Salem,—so that, as you see, my story is at least fourteen miles long. My publisher speaks of it in tremendous terms of approbation ; so does Mrs. Hawthorne, to whom I read the conclusion last night. It broke her heart, and sent her to bed with a grievous headache, which I look upon as a triumphant success."

If Hawthorne was in a sombre mood, and if his future was painfully vague, his book seems, if not to have been born, at least to have shared in his gloomy shadows, for the tragic story is unrelieved by a single ray of sunshine or mitigation of sorrow.

The origin of the poet's *Evangeline* has been thus given in the *Atlantic*:—

" Hawthorne, dining one day with Longfellow, brought with him a friend from Salem. After dinner this friend said, ' I have been trying to persuade Hawthorne to write a story based upon a legend of Acadie, and still current there; the legend of a girl who, in the dispersion of the Acadians, was separated from her lover, and passed her life in waiting and seeking for him, and only found him dying in a hospital, when both were old. Longfellow wondered that this legend did not strike the fancy of Hawthorne, and said to him, ' If you really have made up your mind not to use it for a story, will you give it to me for a poem ? ' To this he assented, and promised not to treat it in prose till Longfellow had seen what he could do with it in verse. "

In his diary, under date of December 6th, 1838, Mr. Longfellow writes :—

" A beautiful holy morning within me. I was

softly excited, I knew not why, and wrote with peace in my heart, and not without tears in my eyes, ' The Reaper and the Flowers, a Psalm of Death.' I have had an idea of this kind in my mind for a long time, without finding any expression for it in words. This morning it seemed to crystallise at once, without any effort of my own.'

"The Skeleton in Armour" was suggested to him, Mr. Longfellow informs us, while he was riding on the seashore at Newport. A year or two previous to his visit a skeleton had been dug up at Fall River, clad in armour, which was corroded and broken; and the idea occurred to the poet of connecting this discovery with the Round Tower at Newport,—generally known hitherto as the Old Windmill, though now claimed by the Danes as a work of their early ancestors. His "Hyperion" and "Voices of the Night" were written at his home in Cambridge. "The Hymn of the Moravian Nuns" he wrote while at college. He says :—

" I read in a newspaper a story that the Moravian women at Bethlehem had embroidered a banner and presented it to Pulaski. The story made an impression upon my mind, and one idle day I wrote the poem. I called them Moravian nuns, because I had gathered from something I had heard or read that they were called nuns. I suppose I should have said Moravian Sisters, but the change does not spoil the romance. I often felt a curiosity to go and see the people whose patriotic action furnished the theme for this poem, and whose peculiar costumes and steady thrift have gained them the admiration of the world."

"The Song of Hiawatha"—an Indian *Edda*—is founded on a tradition prevalent among the North American tribes, of a personage of miraculous birth, who was sent among them to clear their rivers, forests, and fishing-grounds, and to teach them the arts of peace. According to the legend he was known among the different tribes by various names, such as the following,—Michabou, Chiabo, Manabozo, and Hiawatha. Mr. Schoolcraft, in his *Algic Researches*, gives an account of him, derived from the verbal narrations of an Onondaga chief. In Professor Longfellow's poem other curious Indian legends have been interwoven with the above. The scene of the poem is among the Ojibways, on the southern shore of Lake Superior, in the region between the Pictured Rocks and the Grand Sable.

His biographer thus relates the one great tragedy that left its traces on the gentle and beautiful life of the poet :—

"There is a break in the journal here ; and then these lines of Tennyson, added many days after :—

"'Sleep sweetly, tender heart, in peace !
 Sleep, holy spirit, blessed soul !
 While the stars burn, the moons increase,
  And the great ages onward roll.'

"The break in the journal marked a break in his very life ; an awful chasm that suddenly, and without the slightest warning, opened at his feet." [1]

"On July 9th his wife was sitting in the library, with her two little girls, engaged in sealing up some small packages of their curls which she had just cut off. From a match fallen upon the floor her light summer dress caught fire. The shock was too great, and she died the next morning. Three days later her burial took place at Mount Auburn. It was the anniversary of her marriage-day ; and on her beautiful head, lovely and unmarred in death, some hand had placed a wreath

---

[1] Longfellow's *Memoirs of the Poet.*

of orange blossoms. Her husband was not there
—confined to his chamber by the severe burns
which he had himself received.

"These wounds healed with time. Time could
only assuage, never heal, the deeper wounds that
burned within. This terrible bereavement, made
more terrible by the shock of the suddenness and
the manner of it, well-nigh crushed him. Friends
gathered round, and letters of sympathy poured in
upon him from every quarter, as the sad intelligence
flashed over the land and sea. He bore his grief
with courage and in silence. Only after months
had passed could he speak of it ; and then only in
fewest words. To a brother far distant he wrote :
'And now, of what we both are thinking, I can
write no word. God's will be done.' To a
visitor, who expressed the hope that he might be
enabled to 'bear his cross' with patience, he replied : '*Bear* the cross, yes; but what if one is
stretched upon it !'"

Eighteen years after, he wrote these
lines, found in his portfolio after his
death :—

"THE CROSS OF SNOW.

" In the long, sleepless watches of the night,
A gentle form—the face of one long dead—
Looks at me from the wall, where round its
head
A night-lamp casts a halo of pale light.

Here in this room she died ; and soul more
    white
  Never through martyrdom of fire was led
  To its repose ; nor can in books be read
The legend of a life more benedight.
  There is a mountain in the distant west,
That, sun-defying, in its deep ravines
Displays a cross of snow upon its side.
  Such is the cross I wear upon my breast
These eighteen years, through all the changing
    scenes
And seasons, changeless since the day she died."

Longfellow's first printed verses appeared in a local paper, when he was
thirteen. The young poet waited till his
father read his newspaper by the log-fire,
and then with secret triumph found that
the poem was actually printed. That
evening he went with his father to visit
a neighbour, Judge Mellen, and the old
Judge happened to say, " Did you see
the piece in to-day's paper? Very
stiff, remarkably stiff; moreover, it is
all borrowed—every word of it." The
poet of thirteen felt ready to sink
through the floor; but he got away as
soon as he could, without betraying himself. He was crushed but not extinguished

by his first critic. The career that followed
has been sketched by the poet's brother,
with extracts from letters and journals,
enough to make it an autobiography.

" We find the sources of his poetry here, and
are led by the alchemist himself into his laboratory
to watch the secrets of making the gold."

In accordance with the theory of inspiration, it was always a pleasure when a new
poem formed itself rapidly in his mind
and required few emendations. Thus the
famous " Psalm of Life " was hastily jotted
down upon the blank portions of a note
of invitation ; and with reference to the
" Wreck of the Hesperus " he says :—" I
feel pleased with the ballad. It hardly
cost me an effort. It did not come into
my mind by lines, but by stanzas." It
will be remembered that " Tam o'Shanter,"
the masterpiece of Burns, was also dashed
off " at a heat."

Among the poems published after his
death is a touching one called " The
Children's Crusade." It was, unfortunately, left unfinished. It is founded on
an event which occurred in 1212. An

army of twenty thousand children, mostly boys, under the lead of a boy of ten years, named Nicolas, set out from Cologne for the Holy Land. When they reached Genoa, only seven thousand remained. There, as the sea did not divide to allow them to march dry shod to the East, they broke up. Some got as far as Rome; two ship loads sailed from Pisa and were not heard of again; the rest straggled back to Germany.

Poetry has often been defined; here is an excellent definition :—

" Poetry, under her own peculiar laws, is more than any other pursuit of man, perhaps, the direct reflection of the spirit of the age as it passes. The mirror she holds up is not so much to nature at large, as to human nature. The poet is, indeed, the child of his century: his art not only gives back the form and pressure to the body of the time ; but it is itself the impersonation of its most advanced thought, the efflorescence of its finest spirit."[1]

The Autocrat of the Breakfast-table, the most popular production of that popular poet and essayist Dr. Oliver

---

[1] *Quarterly Review.*

Wendell Holmes, as far as can be ascertained, has no legendary story as to its origin. That this very original work should have proved such a great favourite surprises no person who has perused its pleasant and brilliant pages. It has been conjectured that the plan of the work may have been suggested either by the *Noctes Ambrosianæ,* or Boswell's *Life of Johnson ;* but it is safe and, perhaps, sufficient to say that, if modelled after either, it is worthy of both. The gems that are scattered among its pages are evidence enough of the poetic skill and humour of its author.

As the keynote to much of Whittier's poetry, we might, perhaps, take his own quaint and picturesque stanza :—

> "I love the old melodious lays which softly melt
>   the ages through,
>   The songs of Spenser's golden days, Arcadia-
>   Sidney's silver phrase,
>   Sprinkling o'er the noon of time with freshest
>   morning dew."

Whittier's style has been characterised as pure strong Saxon. It is said that he composes many of his beautiful passages while walking, and afterwards commits them to paper. Most of his eloquent anti-slavery appeals were occasioned by the events to which they sometimes refer. We gather a little inkling of his genial and kindly nature in the last verses of one of his poems, entitled "The Reward" :—

"Alas ! the evil which we fain would shun,
  We do, and leave the wished-for good undone !
        Our strength to-day
  Is but to-morrow's weakness, prone to fall,—
  Poor, blind, unprofitable servants all
        Are we alway.

"Yet who, thus looking backward o'er his years,
  Feels not his eyelids wet with grateful tears,
        If he hath been
  Permitted, weak and sinful as he was,
  To cheer and aid, in some ennobling cause,
        His fellow men ?"

We have reason to be proud of this poet-philanthropist, — "his lyre having been struck and attuned to many a stirring note for freedom and human progress," as well as to the high interests of virtue and religion.

Latest, but not least, indeed, in the

illustrious order of the sons of song is the representative poet of England, Lord Tennyson, the Poet-Laureate, who has been justly characterised as "the incarnate voice of cultivated and refined England, in his time." An estimate endorsed by another acknowledged authority,[1] who says :—

"No one else has the same combination of melody, beauty of description, culture, and intellectual power. He has sweetness and strength in exquisite combination. If a just balance of poetic powers were to be crown of a poet, then undoubtedly Tennyson must be proclaimed the greatest English poet of our time."

It would be, of course, superfluous to call attention to the earlier productions of his muse,—" The May Queen," " Locksley Hall," " Maud," "The Idylls of the King," "The Princess," "The Lady of Shalott," and others,—since they are familiar to all lovers of true poetry. But it may be well to cite a word or two from Charles Kingsley respecting his fine philosophical poem in memory of his friend Hallam. He says :—

[1] Justin McCarthy.

" We know not whether to envy more the poet, the object of his admiration, or the monument which he has consecrated to his nobleness. In this poem, written at various intervals during a series of years, all the poet's peculiar excellences, with all he has acquired from others, seem to have been fused into a perfect unity, and brought to bear on the subject, with that care and finish which only a labour of love can inspire."

And should there be need for further tribute, we have these enthusiastic words from Mr. Gladstone. Referring to " The Idylls of the King," he says :—

" No one can read this poem without feeling, when it ends, what may be termed the pangs of vacancy—of that void in heart and mind for want of its continuance of which we are conscious when some noble strain of music ceases, when some great work of Raphael passes from view, when we lose sight of some spot connected with high associations, or when some transcendent character upon the page of history disappears,—and the withdrawal of it is like the withdrawal of the vital air."

Should we not, then, cherish with loving regard these treasured legacies of the lyre, and hold in high esteem those who have so nobly enriched our literature, and imparted to our too prosaic life such a revenue of intellectual enjoyment? Finally, if a nation's glory and renown may be said to depend in great part upon its authors and artists, then no logic is needed to enforce their claims upon its grateful esteem and lasting remembrance.

" The pen hath ruled with regal sway
The conquering sword,—and crowned its way !
Like Phœbus, with Promethean fire,—
Jove's thunder and Apollo's lyre,—
Its diamond point, like stars at night,
Hath turned earth's shadows into light ! "

INDEX.

The Book=Lover's Library.

EDITED BY

HENRY B. WHEATLEY, F.S.A.

Tastefully printed on antique paper, handsomely bound in
cloth; also on handmade paper, Roxburgh binding, and
50 only large paper copies for collectors.

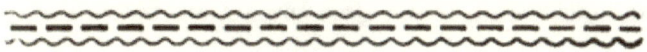

THE DEDICATION of BOOKS To PATRON and FRIEND.

By HENRY B. WHEATLEY, F.S.A.

Being the Fifth Volume of "The Book-Lover's
Library."

Contents.

"Throughout Mr. Wheatley has done his work
thoroughly and in a most judicious way. There is a
good index, highly necessary to such a book, which is
certainly worthy of a place in every good library."

Public Opinion.

14

MODERN METHODS

ᵒᶜ

ILLUSTRATING BOOKS.

"The various styles of illustration and the transition from the one to the other, with all the most notable peculiarities of each, from the old woodcuts down to the photogravure of yesterday, are set forth in a graphic and interesting form."—*Warrington Guardian.*

HOW to FORM a LIBRARY.

By H. B. WHEATLEY, F.S.A.

Being the First Volume of "The Book-Lovers Library."

Contents.

HOW MEN HAVE FORMED LIBRARIES.	GENERAL BIBLIOGRAPHIES.
HOW TO BUY.	SPECIAL BIBLIOGRAPHIES.
PUBLIC LIBRARIES.	PUBLISHING SOCIETIES.
PRIVATE LIBRARIES.	CHILD'S LIBRARY.
	ONE HUNDRED BOOKS.

"An admirable guide to the best bibliographies and books of reference. . . . It is altogether a volume to be desired."—*Globe.*

"Everything about this book is satisfactory—paper, type, margin, size, above all, the contents."

St. James's Gazette.

"Supplies in a compact form much that the librarian and book-lover could not obtain elsewhere without lengthy research."—*Oxford Chronicle.*

THE LITERATURE of LOCAL INSTITUTIONS.

By G. LAURENCE GOMME, F.S.A.

The work is divided into the following sections :—

1. LOCAL GOVERNMENT GENERALLY.
2. THE SHIRE.
3. THE HUNDRED.
4. THE MUNICIPAL BOROUGH
5. THE GUILDS.
6. THE MANOR.
7. THE TOWNSHIP AND PARISH.

"A handy and useful guide to the study of a vast subject. The writer's experience in bibliography and index-making is fully reflected in the descriptive list of works appended to each section of an excellent exposition of the antiquity and growth of local institutions."—*Saturday Review.*

⊕

OLD COOKERY BOOKS and ANCIENT CUISINE.

By W. C. HAZLITT.

"This is a book of pleasant gossip on a subject which is not easily exhausted, and can hardly fail to be interesting."—*Spectator.*

"It will be found very pleasant reading alike by the bibliophilist, the scholarly cook, and those interested in gastronomy."—*Hotel Review.*

"Mr. Hazlitt has produced a thoroughly entertaining and clever little book, full of curious facts relating to the food of past generations, and its mode of preparation for the table."—*Bookseller.*

"Full of curious information, this work can fairly claim to be a philosophical history of our national cookery."—*Morning Post.*

GLEANINGS in OLD GARDEN LITERATURE.

By W. C. HAZLITT.

In this new volume of the BOOK-LOVER'S LIBRARY the author has gleaned in many out-of-the-way fields, and has brought home and spread before the reader a banquet well garnished with fruit and vegetable lore, rendered pleasant by the fragrance of many old-fashioned flowers. The illustrious men of our country who have delighted in a country life, and have spent their leisure hours in the pleasures of the garden, sit round the board, while some of the great gardeners enliven their patrons with curious narratives of their craft in pleasant fashion.

Contents.

"A volume that may afford delight to the lover of gardens, even if he be not a lover of books in general."

Morning Post.